I0739380

# More Than Instinct

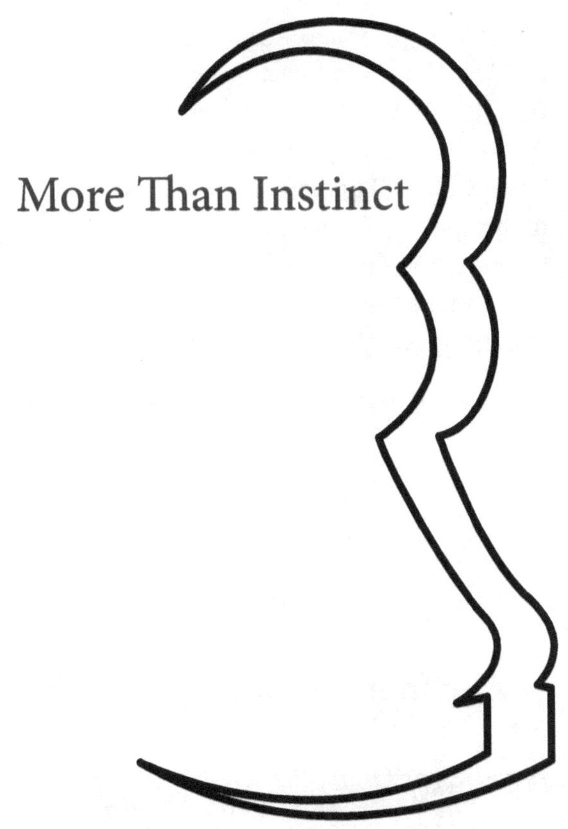

# Available from Elizabeth Lee Sorrell

*Wrong Turn Fairy Tales*

Gwynn worked hard to live up to her family's expectations putting away all childish things and even a few childhood friends. Now she is about to marry Addison, a very sensible, very rich businessman, but before she can say yes to his proposal, she finds herself falling through one fairy tale after another. Will  she find her happily ever after with her very own prince charming, or has her fairy tale taken a wrong turn?

Exclusively found from Barnes & Nobles for Nook Book.

# Also from our Author... Children's Books

*Sugar Sugar On a Stick*

Who doesn't love a good lollipop? Is it possible to love them too much? What would you do with the power to magically create lollipops? One little girl finds out, but will the cost be worth the sugary prize?

# More Than Instinct

*Elizabeth Lee Sorrell*

trading as

Yarbrough House Publishing

*Acknowledgements*


I'd like to thank my family who really do all the hard work. While I sit back and make up fanciful stories, my family stays busy proofing, formatting, illustrating, crunching numbers, and taking care of all the "business stuff." All I do is play with my imagination, but my family works hard to bring life to my stories.

## Fifteen Years Earlier

"Why do you have to go to Kansas anyway?" Jeb asked.

"My aunt has a baby in her stomach," Melissa answered.

"Ewww, gross! Why did your aunt swallow a baby?" Jeb asked.

"She didn't swallow a baby, silly," Melissa responded.

"Then how did a baby get in her stomach?" Jeb asked.

"Mama said that's just what happens sometimes when two people get married," Melissa explained.

"Do you think that's going to happen to Suzie?" Jeb asked.

"I think so. What was Suzie's boyfriend's name?" Melissa asked.

"Deek or something like that," Jeb answered.

"I know they'll have the same last name after they get married," Melissa pointed out.

"I don't know his last name, but I know he's not her boyfriend anymore," Jeb said.

"Why not?"

"Everyone keeps calling him her fiancé now," Jeb answered.

"Oh… Jeb, how long to you think we'll love each other?" Melissa wondered.

"Forever I guess."

"Do you think we'll have to get married too?"

"Probably so."

"How long do you think we have?"

"I don't know," Jeb admitted.

"How old is Suzie?" Melissa asked.

"I don't know exactly. I know she's thirteen years older than me," Jeb replied.

"Well, that makes it easy then. We have to get married in thirteen years. You really should know how old your sister is," Melissa said.

"Fine, thirteen plus seven is twenty. Suzie is twenty years old. That makes Deek twenty-two, so maybe we can wait until we're twenty-two," Jeb added.

"You'll be twenty-two before me," Melissa pointed out.

"It's only two months, but we can wait until you're twenty-two. Will I get a baby in my stomach too?" Jeb worried.

"No, it's just the mommies."

"Good, I don't want a baby in my stomach. It sounds awful."

"I'm not scared," Melissa declared.

"Really?" Jeb asked. Melissa shook her head boldly. "Suzie and Deek have to live together after they get married. If you're not scared, we should get married now. That way we have to be together no matter where they make us go," Jeb suggested.

"How? We don't even know how to get married," Melissa noted.

"We will after we watch Suzie and Deek get married," Jeb replied.

"OK, but we should wait until the day we go to see my aunt, and we can't tell anyone. That way it will be too late for them to stop us," Melissa plotted.

Jeb agreed, and they began their plotting.

# Chapter 1

Fifteen years later… "Well look at this! I finally got you both here and for the same trip at that," Mrs. Judy exclaimed. "Kat, how is your aunt doing? I heard she was sick last week."

"She's feeling much better, thank you."

"Good, good. Kat this is Jackson. He's helping out at the courthouse on a temporary basis. He's been in town two months. He's been attending our church every Sunday, but this is the first time he's done anything with the single's group. I'm so glad he finally joined us. Jackson, this is Kat. She's been attending our church with her aunt since she was what eight or nine?" Mrs. Judy said looking at Kat.

"Seven," Kat interjected.

"She's a local teacher. She teaches third grade. She's kind of quiet at first, but that wont last long. She is one of the sweetest people I know. I'm sure you two will get along just fine. If you'll excuse me, I've got to make sure that I get an accurate head count," Mrs. Judy said, and she walked off leaving Jackson and Kat standing alone.

Jackson was somewhat tall. Kat was not short herself. She stood tall for a girl at five-ten, but Jackson stood at least four inches above Kat. He had dark, brown hair and even darker, brown eyes. His eyes were so dark that at first glance they appeared black. His complexion was a perfect golden brown. His physique was the kind only seen on TV or on male models, with every muscle well defined and his well honed six pack hinted at behind his T-shirt. He had an almost herculean build.

Kat had dark, green eyes, and her olive toned skin matched her beautiful eyes gloriously. Her clear complexion showed off her naturally blushed cheeks. Her brown hair was light-colored in contrast to Jackson's dark, brown. It flowed softly down her back with a silky shine. She carried herself well and had a flawless figure, full of curves that were not at all hidden behind her conservative clothes.

"So where did you move from?" Kat asked.

"No where in particular. I move around a lot. In fact, I rarely live in one place more than a year," Jackson answered.

Kat gave a slight nod. It was a vague answer, not one that lent itself to conversation. "I bet the courthouse is interesting. What do you do?" she asked.

"A little bit of everything," Jackson answered shortly. It was clear by the look on Jackson's face that he was not interested in the conversation and intended to terminate it immediately.

"OK… Are you always so friendly?" Kat asked.

"Are you always so nervous?" Jackson returned.

"I didn't say I was nervous," Kat pointed out.

"I didn't say I wasn't friendly either. Some things are just obvious, like the way you keep shifting your weight, short rapid breathing, your eyes keep darting around, and you're fidgeting with your shirt tail. Why so nervous teach?" Jackson asked.

"You're observant… To be perfectly honest with you, I wasn't sure if you were in on the match up with Mrs. Judy. I don't like being fixed up, especially when I'm being blind sided," Kat explained.

"Let me put your mind at ease, teach. I don't do blind anything. I like having more control than that," Jackson said.

"So you're a control freak," Kat commented.

"In a way," Jackson snarled. This woman was really making his blood boil. He hadn't known her more than five minutes, and she was already grating on his nerves. She was offensive to say the very least, quiet at first nothing.

"There is a problem with the bus," Mrs. Judy said interrupting the tension. "We are going to have to take two vans. I'm going to take my van, and Jenny is going to drive the church van. Kat, you simply must ride with me. I want to hear all about how school is going this year."

Mrs. Judy was a retired principal and widowed into the singles group. She was shorter than both Kat and Jackson. She was five-four at most and very pale. She was almost white when compared to Kat and Jackson's natural tan. Her silver hair was curled and cut short. Her small, tight lips sat deep on her wrinkled face. Her small frame had basically no curves left.

"Great, I want to ask you about something anyway," Kat replied.

"In that case, I'll ride in the church van," Jackson said coldly and started off toward the church van.

"What was that about?" Mrs. Judy asked as they climbed into the van followed by six other singles.

"I'd like to ask you the same thing," Kat responded.

"What do you mean?" Mrs. Judy asked.

"Mrs. Judy…"

"OK, OK. I've been trying to get you two together for a long while now. So what did you think?" Mrs. Judy asked. Mrs. Judy's eagerness could not have been more apparent. Her face lit up with curiousness and excitement. It made Kat wonder just how long a long while had been.

"I thought he was extremely rude," Kat admitted.

"Really? Maybe he's having a bad day. He really is polite once you get to know him. He's also a very private man. He doesn't open up easy, and even then he doesn't reveal much. Give it time. I'm sure you two will hit it off. Now, tell me all about school," Mrs. Judy insisted.

Once a girl hits a certain age without getting married, it is assumed by everyone that she must need help finding someone. For Kat that certain age was thirty-three. For two years everyone had been trying to fix Kat up. Kat was set up by her aunt, by friends, by colleagues, and even by other members of the singles group, including Mrs. Judy. Kat had been set up with a wide variety of guys. The so called match makers had set her up with their friends, their family, their acquaintances, their colleagues. Kat hated being set up. She had been on more bad dates than she cared to count. Nothing good had ever come from being fixed up. Kat had begged everyone numerous times not to fix her up no matter how perfect a match they thought they had found. Obviously all her begging was for not.

"School is wonderful," Kat said.

"Of course it is. School is always wonderful the first month. You haven't had time to get frustrated with behavior problems yet. The children haven't had time to get bored yet. No one gets burned out the first month of school, so everything stays a bed of roses. Kat, you are only two weeks into the year. Be honest. Do you have any students that you see becoming major discipline problems?" Mrs. Judy asked.

"Not at all," Kat answered. "I have one boy who is a little smart mouthed, but not really in a defiant way. It is more of a comical smartness. That is his goal anyway. I have never fallen in love with a group of kids this fast. I have some real brilliant kids too. They are all so eager to learn."

"Of course they are. Everyone is eager this early in the year. I am excited for you, Kat. It sounds like it is going to be a great year," Mrs. Judy agreed. Mrs. Judy had a way of being completely straight forward with teachers but still remain optimistic. That was only one of the things that had made her a great principal for so many, many years. She didn't beat around the bush. She didn't sugar coat. She didn't baby anyone, but she made them feel like everything would be OK, everything could be improved.

"I think so," Kat said.

The singles group was headed to Atlanta for a Braves game. There were many baseball fans in their group, and they were out for one last hurrah of the season. Judy being ever sneaky and resourceful, managed to fix it that Kat and Jackson sat next to each other once they got to the stadium, but all her effort was for nothing. Jackson had a very stiff demeanor. He apparently enjoyed the game, and he did not need anyone's help to occupy himself. Kat, on the other hand, had never been interested much in sports. The guy sitting to her right was tortuously boring and slightly annoying, but Kat would do almost anything at this point to avoid Jackson.

For three hours Kat made pointless and sometimes confusing conversation with the guy next to her. At one point he rambled on for about five minutes about something that made no sense at all and then burst out in high-pitched, squealing laughter. Kat could have sworn she saw a smirk spread across Jackson's face.

Jackson tried to focus his full attention on the game, but the guy on Kat's other side was rambunctious and loud. Jackson honestly wasn't sure if he had fried his brain on drugs or some other nonsense or if he really was born this stupid. Jackson couldn't help but sneak a peak in their direction when the guy started giggling like a school girl loud enough to be heard throughout the entire section of seating. The guy had his eyes scrunched closed as he keeled over laughing. Kat looked stunned, unsure how to react. Jackson repressed a smile and turned back to the game which really wasn't half as much fun as that stunned expression on Kat's face.

Kat and Jackson never said more than two words to one another throughout the entire game, but Mrs. Judy is a very determined woman and had nothing better to do since she retired. It seemed that the name of the game was match making, and Mrs. Judy was not one to throw in the towel; she did not know the meaning of the word quit.

# Chapter 2

The next scheduled activity for the singles group was game night the following Saturday night. "Jackson, you're late," Mrs. Judy called out as Jackson walked in the door. "That's OK. We haven't gotten started over here yet. I hear your favorite board game is Clue. It's Kat's favorite too. She's virtually unstoppable. Come on over here. See if you can match Kat's skills."

Not having much of a choice since everyone else had already started, Jackson walked over and sat down next to Mrs. Judy across from Kat. The game started out slow as usual while everyone tried to collect their clues and read each others' reactions.

"Scarlet, in the kitchen, with the revolver," Jackson accused only shortly into the game.

"Are you serious? You're making an accusation already?" the man next to Kat asked. Kat narrowed her eyes suspiciously. She already had the idea that he was right, but no one answered that quickly into a game.

Jackson did not respond. He just smiled. "Are you sure you're ready to accuse?" Mrs. Judy asked sweetly.

"Positive," Jackson answered.

Mrs. Judy opened up the envelope and pulled out the cards. Scarlet… Kitchen… Revolver. "Not bad," Kat commented softly.

"Not bad? Teach, that was skill. How did I match up?" Jackson retorted with an annoying wink.

"I underestimated you. It won't happen again," Kat replied smartly.

They played three more rounds of which Kat won all three. She wasn't holding back anymore. If he wanted to play that fast and furious, two could play at that game. Both Kat and Jackson were overly competitive. Most people tolerated Kat's competitiveness with mild amusement, but that was before she had someone else around as competitive as herself. Now people were slightly uncomfortable. They must have been secretly wondering which one would explode first.

Later game nights, proved Kat and Jackson to be pretty evenly matched but at each other's throats. Neither would choose another game, and although everyone else playing always had fun, Kat and Jackson made each other miserable, each trying to out do the other. In their own twisted way, though, Kat and Jackson somehow enjoyed playing clue, battling against one another every game night.

Game night was not the only time of uneasiness. No matter where or what the situation, the tension was obvious anytime Kat and Jackson were near each other. The tension could almost be cut with a knife.

Kat and Jackson sat on opposite sides of the sanctuary to avoid contact. Sunday School, however, was another story. The singles Sunday School room was tiny, and an average of twelve people stuffed themselves in the tiny room. This left Kat and Jackson with few options. They either minimized the space between them, or they could sit on opposite sides of the room, sitting across from one another in tiny quarters

It was always little things that set Kat and Jackson off. Kat thought Jackson was too nosey. Jackson thought Kat was too nonchalant. Kat thought Jackson was too bossy. Jackson thought Kat was too laid back. Kat thought Jackson was rude. Jackson thought Kat was a push over. A single look could start the bickering. A simple comment or lack of comment could set off a battering of harsh combative comments back and forth.

Kat and Jackson simply had a personality clash. Jackson was a strong take charge type. Kat was a gentle loving type. Both were strong willed and bold; this is what really caused them to butt heads. Each one thought that their way was better and would not back down.

Kat and Jackson were unable to complete a single task without bickering. They were not necessarily violent; they just continued in a constant squabble with one another. They fought like kids.

The second weekend in December the singles group planned a trip to view Christmas lights. Mrs. Judy and a few others were at the church a little early, just trying to pass time while they waited. Mrs. Judy asked, "Jackson, I heard you were working at S & R Offices. Is it true?"

"Yes, ma'am," Jackson answered.

Kat rolled her eyes. "What happened? Did you lose your job? Weren't you working at the bank just last week? That's the third job you've had in five months. Can't you keep a job?"

"What is your problem?" Jackson shot back. "No one was even talking to you. It is none of your business anyway, but just for the record, I've never been fired from anything a day in my life. I quit every one of those jobs of my own free will, and I will quit as many more as I please."

Kat rolled her eyes again. Jackson seemed dependable when it came to different stuff around church, but how dependable was he really if he up and left jobs on a whimsy? Talk about a major loyalty default.

"Now what?" Jackson asked.

"I didn't say anything," Kat answered.

"You thought it; you might as well come out with it," Jackson said.

"It's nothing. You just don't sound dependable. That's all," Kat replied.

"Now, Kat," Mrs. Judy interrupted, "you know I hate to getting in the middle, but that just isn't true. Jackson is a very dependable young man."

Kat and Jackson were still staring each other down. Both seemed to be daring the other to make a move.

"She knows that it's not true," Jackson told Mrs. Judy calmly. "Don't you?" he urged Kat. He had more than proved to this singles group that he could be depended on. Even Kat couldn't deny that. "That would be like me saying that because she is such a pushover, she must be a lousy teacher." She was a pushover. She let everyone push her around. She clearly didn't want to be set up on blind dates, but she didn't stop anyone from doing it. She voiced her disapproval and let them go on setting her up. Her time was stretched thin as it was, but she was always the first people went to when they needed a task done or a job filled, because she did not know how to say no.

"Is that what you think?" Kat asked.

"Of course not," Jackson answered. The fact that she was such a pushover was irrelevant to her effectiveness as a teacher. Although, Jackson was assuming that her students did not run her over like the adults in her life.

"Things aren't always what they seem, are they?" Kat commented dryly.

"Rarely are," Jackson replied.

"You two are too much for me," Mrs. Judy said as she turned and walked away.

Kat and Jackson continued to stare each other down another minute or two. There was something rather strange about Jackson. He was secretive, too secretive as far as Kat was concerned. He was not a shy person, did not pretend to be, but he kept so much to himself. He was a prime example of things not always being what they seemed.

The way Jackson watched people was strange as well. He looked at people as if he was constantly sizing them up. He was not an overly trusting person; he observed people like he was suspicious of everyone. There was something up with him. Jackson was not at all what he seemed or maybe who he seemed.

"Is there something you needed to talk to me about?" Jackson asked.

"Not particularly," Kat replied.

"Then let's go," Jackson said turning toward the bus. Kat followed him onto the bus without a word. Kat sat down in the first seat while Jackson moved on back. He sat down about mid-way back.

The trip went smoothly (mainly because Kat and Jackson were too far apart to argue). Everyone had a blast. The lights were brilliant, colorful, and beautiful. They lit up the night and set a cheerful mood. All the red and green everywhere and manger scenes really put everyone in the Christmas spirit.

For the next couple weeks Mrs. Judy stayed on both Kat and Jackson to get a date for the single group's New Year's Eve party. Part of her still wanted them to go together, but for the most part she had come to grips with the fact that it was never going to happen. Although they had a lot in common, they would neither ever admit to that. They both refused to get along. Of course by the New Year's Eve, neither one had a date. The party started at eight; Kat and Jackson did a good job of avoiding each other until just after ten. Kat was sitting outside on the front steps when Jackson walked out.

"Kat, you don't have a date," Jackson taunted. He couldn't miss the chance for a good ribbing. She was sitting alone on the front steps looking miserable. Really, she was making it too easy.

"Neither do you," Kat reminded him.

"What are you doing out here?" Jackson asked.

"Just sulking, I guess," Kat admitted.

"Why do that? You sulk too much. Take action. Change things," Jackson said.

"That's easy for you to say," Kat retorted.

"Yeah, it is. I don't sit around sulking. It should be easy for you too. What are you sulking about anyway?" Jackson asked.

"Do you always have to ask so many questions?" Kat asked.

"Yes, it's habit I suppose," Jackson answered. "So what are you doing out here?"

It is a habit to ask a bunch of questions, Kat wondered. She thought that was a little strange, but she ignored it for now. "Did you not notice? We are the only two here tonight under sixty without dates," Kat pointed out. "It is sort of pathetic."

"I did notice. We are pretty pathetic. In my defense, I didn't expect to make it tonight," Jackson replied.

It was apparent in his expression that he was expecting something more exciting. He looked disappointed in a way.

Kat gave Jackson a funny, thoughtful look. "Is there something else?" Jackson asked.

"I don't think so," Kat responded. That was a lie. There was something else, something big. There was always something peculiar about Jackson, almost suspicious. Tonight he could easily snap on anyone who gave him a reason. He was wound too tightly. It was like he was just itching for a fight and not just arguing with her. He wanted someone who he could throw punches with. Kat desperately wanted to ask Jackson what his big secret was. Her curiosity was getting the best of her. The suspense was almost more than she could bear, but she was also afraid that as soon as she found out, she would regret asking. This man was not a simple game of clue. Whatever secret he was hiding could very well change everything in the blink of an eye, maybe even threaten her safety. "Anyway, that's why I had to get out for a while. Why did you come out here?" Kat asked.

"Well to be honest, this is kind of lame considering what I thought I'd be doing tonight," Jackson admitted bluntly. Lame was putting it mildly, he thought. Jackson was expecting a fight, a fight to the death if necessary. He was looking for a way out, a means to an end. He was ready for this whole thing to be over, but it was far from over and only getting more complicated by the day.

Kat smiled and looked at Jackson accusingly. She had to agree with him on that point. The party was rather lame. Kat could think of at least a dozen other things that she could be doing tonight that would be more fun. Kat had a very strong feeling that she and Jackson were not longing for the same type of fun, and Kat had an even stronger feeling that told her she did not need to know what type of fun Jackson longed for.

"What?" Jackson laughed.

"Nothing," Kat said.

"Are you sure you don't have something else on your mind?" Jackson urged.

"Positive," Kat insisted.

"OK, suit yourself," Jackson gave in as he sat down next to Kat on the stairs. He looked around, took a deep breath, and let it out slowly. "Why do you teach?" he asked genuinely curious about her motivation to work with young children.

"I like teaching. It's my passion. I love the children and watching them grow up over the course of a year.

It's amazing to watch how much knowledge they retain over the year and to know that I taught them that. I get the chance to teach them not only school lessons but life lessons as well. I become a part of their lives that can't be replaced or erased. It's up to me to be sure I'm a positive part of their lives, that I make a positive impact. It's so wonderful. I mean it's an indescribable feeling. It's awesome," Kat explained.

"And you like it?" Jackson asked with a grin. Kat was without doubt the most aggravating person he knew, but she had a good heart.

"Do you have to be so aggravating?" Kat asked, but Jackson's grin never faded. "What about you?" she asked.

"What about me?" Jackson responded.

"Do you like what you do? What do you do at S & R Offices anyway?" Kat asked.

"Oh not much of anything. A little bit of everything. I do a little of this and a little of that. I run errands. I draw out plans. I look over rough drafts. I've even been known to answer phones from time to time," Jackson replied.

"Do you like that?" Kat asked.

"Yeah, for now," Jackson answered.

"For now," Kat mocked rolling her eyes. "What about all the job hopping you do? You never have a stable plan. Do like that?"

"Oh yeah! I love what I do. It's exciting. I'm constantly trying something new. I never stay in one place long enough to get bored. Since I never get into a rut, I am forced to use my head on a daily basis; you know, really stretch my brain and see how far I can get. You never know what you're capable of until you're pushed to the limits," Jackson explained. That was as honest as he had been with anyone in years. He loved all the role playing he did.

"You may have a point when you put it that way, but don't you think that there are just some boundaries or limits that shouldn't be crossed?" Kat asked.

"Some boundaries were made to be crossed; others depend on the situation. What kind of boundaries, and why are you crossing them?" Jackson returned with a question, but Kat never got the time to answer.

Mrs. Judy opened the door. "I've been looking for you two every where. What are you doing out here? It's freezing. Come on. It's almost midnight, and I'm not going to let you two miss ringing in the new year because you were outside catching pneumonia," she said, and she practically drug Kat and Jackson back inside.

Kat and Jackson went quietly and retreated to opposite corners. They did not talk again until almost Valentine's Day.

# Chapter 3

Every year the singles group has a Valentine's banquet the weekend before Valentine's, and this year Kat had an actual date for the banquet. He was a tall, blonde man. He was a big, strong, very intimidating man. He had been a blind date, what else, but it had worked out better this time. The man was polite and interesting. Kat did not mind spending time with him; in fact, she actually enjoyed spending time with him. He was fun.

Afterwards Kat, Mrs. Judy, Jackson, and two others volunteered to stay and clean up.

"Kat, tell me about that guy I saw you with tonight," Mrs. Judy nudged.

Kat smiled. "His name is Kelley White," she started.

"His name is Kelley?" Jackson asked half teasingly, half in disbelief.

"Don't start," Kat warned.

"I didn't say a word. I was only asking if I heard correctly," Jackson defended, but he would have if given half a chance. He already didn't like the guy. Jackson had taken one look at the guy strolling in on Kat's arm and taken an immediate dislike to him.

"Yeah, well," Kat said rolling her eyes, "stay out of it."

"Jackson, shush," Mrs. Judy instructed. "I want to hear about this guy. Kat, go on. What does he do?"

"He's a cop," Kat answered.

"Humph," Jackson mumbled under his breath. Great, another chump.

Kat cut her eyes over at Jackson and continued. "He's thirty-three, originally from Kentucky. He moved here four months ago. He's been visiting churches, but he's coming here Sunday."

"That's great," Mrs. Judy said encouragingly.

"Did you notice anything funny about that guy?" Jackson asked.

"I know what you're talking about," Kat responded quickly. She knew that Jackson was at least every bit as observant as she was, and it was the first thing that she had noticed. "He's divorced. That's why there is a tan line from the ring."

Jackson rolled his eyes. "Yeah, right. How long?" Jackson inquired. It couldn't have been too long if he still had the tan line.

"Five months," Kat answered.

"Sure, whatever. I've got to get these tables put up," Jackson said. He had not had that ring off for five months. Jackson did not believe he'd had it off for a full month, but there was no sense in telling Kat that. She wouldn't listen anyway.

"I wish you would," Kat commented.

"Don't pay him any mind, Kat. I think it's wonderful. If you can finish getting these tablecloths, I'm going to go help them with the dishes, so we can get out of here," Mrs. Judy offered.

Kelley joined the church the first Sunday in March. By the end of March he was a consistent member of the singles group. He was involved in every event with the singles group.

Kelley was not wild about Clue, but Kat finally convinced him to join their regular Clue game on game nights. Unfortunately he was very little competition for Kat or Jackson, so the game continued to be dominated by only Kat and Jackson.

"White, I thought this game would be easy, you being a cop and all," Jackson said slyly. For as much as

Kat and Jackson bickered, the rivalry was much worse between Kelley and Jackson. Jackson and Kat had a constant bickering, but Jackson and Kelley had an underlying physical hostility. Neither Kat nor Jackson would ever consider being violent with the other. Jackson kept his cool for the most part, so most people never saw what Kat saw. Jackson hated Kelley for some reason, and Kat knew it.

Jackson tried not to let Kelley get to him, but Kelley just worked his nerves worse than Kat ever could. Jackson had seen his type before. Kelley was a know it all cop, no doubt the kind who would only get in the way in bigger investigations. He worked small time crime scenes and thought he was a big shot. His cockiness was not mere confidence; it was full blown arrogance.

As much as Jackson hated to admit it, Kelley was not right for Kat. He would have loved to have watched them both suffer with each other, but Kat was smarter than that. If Kelley stuck around for much longer, Kat most definitely would not put up with him for much longer. That was a big if; Jackson knew he would not stay for good. It would not be long before Kelley ran back to Kentucky and the woman he had left behind. The only question now was who would leave who first.

At least for the time being, Jackson got the chance to watch them both squirm.

"Alright, big mouth, let's see you win one tonight before you talk about anyone," Kat dared.

"You got it, hot shot," Jackson accepted.

"You make playing a simple board game excruciatingly uncomfortable," a bold young boy named Ben proclaimed. "This is a church sponsored activity. Can't you two chill? At least talk about something else or quit glaring across the table like you could kill one another… So, Kelley, you and Kat are getting pretty serious, huh?" he asked trying to change the subject.

"Oh… um… well, I uh… I don't want to rush into anything at this point. You know what I mean?" Kelley stuttered out awkwardly.

"The Easter music is really coming along in choir. The Easter Cantata will be wonderful this year," Mrs. Judy interrupted.

Jackson looked over at Kat and grinned. Kat cut her eyes across the table. Jackson responded by winking at her. Mrs. Judy gave both of them a stern look and asked, "Whose turn is it?"

Kat knew what Jackson had seen, because she saw it too. Kat saw it often; Kelley just was not ready to move on. Kat knew that it would take time. Kelley had been through a very messy divorce. Kat was understanding, but just the same, she preferred Jackson not know anything about it.

Kat and Jackson put a stop to their silent bickering. No one mentioned Kelley and Kat's relationship again, and everyone's head got back into the game.

Kelley made some lame excuse a little later and left early. Mrs. Judy reluctantly agreed to take Kat home. He is a dreadful liar, Jackson thought. How could anyone in law enforcement be so bad at simple role playing? I cannot believe Ben called Kelley out like that, Jackson marveled, but the looks on their faces were priceless. Kelley looked scared senseless, and he was so jumpy that he would come unglued if someone whispered the word boo. It is tempting, but I have to pass. Kat looked mortified but not surprised. I cannot pass up the opportunity to throw this one back at her later on, Jackson schemed.

"Kat?" Jackson said in a taunting voice.

"Shut up," Kat ordered.

"Your boyfriend is a little jumpy, isn't he?" Jackson asked.

Mrs. Judy cleared her throat. "Jackson, I heard S & R Offices is about to go under. Is there any truth to it?" she asked.

"Is that what you heard?" Jackson replied.

"That's what I heard," Mrs. Judy said.

"Well, we should all know soon enough, I guess," Jackson added.

"Listen, I've got to get up early in the morning. You two live so close; it would be a huge favor to me if you could give Kat a ride home. She's on your way. Do you think that the two of you could make it that far without killing each other first?" Mrs. Judy asked seriously.

"There is no sense in leaving her here. I'll do it for you, Mrs. Judy," Jackson agreed. Kat made no objections although she wanted desperately to do so.

Jackson did not last long once they got into the car. "What was up with that?" he asked.

"What was up with what?" Kat asked.

"You know what," Jackson responded.

"Drop it," Kat snapped.

"White was real jumpy when your relationship was brought up. Then all of the sudden he had to leave in a big hurry, leaving you stranded," Jackson persisted.

"You would be pretty jumpy too. He has been divorced less than a year," Kat defended.

"Not quite, Kat. Reluctance shows fear; jumpiness proves something to hide," Jackson explained.

"What is your point?" Kat asked.

"He's hiding something," Jackson answered.

"I think I would know. Can we talk about something else?" Kat responded. He was hiding something. Kat knew that and had a pretty positive idea what he was hiding, but she would not admit that to Jackson.

"We don't have to talk at all," Jackson offered.

"What will you do if S & R Offices do go under?" Kat asked trying to change the subject.

"Oh, you know. I'll just follow my instincts. See where I get pulled next," Jackson answered.

Kat gave Jackson an almost accusing look. "Do you have something to ask me?" Jackson asked.

"Nope, nothing at all," Kat replied.

"Ask me," Jackson ordered. She knew. Jackson had no idea yet how much she knew, but she had to know something. She was always giving him those annoyingly knowing looks.

"I have nothing to ask," Kat insisted.

"Just ask and get it over with. We both know what you want to ask," Jackson said.

"I don't want to ask. I think I already know the answer, and believe me, I don't want to know. The less I know, the better off we both are," Kat reacted.

Kat knew that there was more going on with Jackson than he let on. Of that she was already positive, but she could not be positive what was going on. He definitely had a secret, a big one. He was hiding something, but was it even legal? Jackson was not what Kat would consider a bad person, annoying but not bad. Whatever he was involved in, his intentions were good, but how much danger was he really in? Why else would he keep such a big secret?

"You're right about that," Jackson relented. "So what do you want to do now?"

"I want to continue just the way things are. We avoid the subject. We avoid each other," Kat answered.

Kat did not really believe that Jackson was involved in something illegal, but it was big and probably complicated. Whatever it was, Kat wanted no part of it.

"Sounds perfect," Jackson agreed if only she would quit looking at him as if she could see right through him.

# Chapter 4

Kat and Jackson avoided each other well for a while. They talked very little at church functions, and they never ran into each other at any other time.

The first Saturday night in May, Kat was sitting at a table in a sports bar and grill when Jackson sat down across from her.

It was a small place just outside of town. The decor was lousy, but the food was excellent. The bartender made a fabulous strawberry daiquiri. The best part was that not many people knew about this particular hole in the wall. It was not usually crowded. It was a place Kat could come to be alone when she wanted to think. "What are you doing here?" she asked.

"That's just what I wanted to know. We both know you have a pretty good idea what drove me here tonight, so what drove you here tonight?" Jackson asked.

"This," Kat said slamming a folded sheet of paper down on the table. She didn't know what had brought Jackson there to that particular sports bar alone, only that it must have something to do with his big secret, but frankly, she didn't care.

Jackson looked at Kat thoughtfully a second or two before he picked up the paper. Kat was clearly upset about something. Jackson was not sure that he really wanted to get involved. Whatever was on that paper was personal and upsetting, at least to Kat. Jackson did not want any part of that, but he did need an excuse to be there. Conversation with Kat was the perfect excuse to be there, and Kat was positioned perfectly. Jackson could not have planned it any better. He carefully unfolded the paper. Dear Kat, he read silently. We both knew that we couldn't last. Let's face it. It's time we called it quits. I'm going back home to Kentucky. The short note had obviously been written in a rush. Kelley had not even taken the time to sign it. "Ouch," Jackson mumbled.

"He's going back to his ex-wife," Kat grumbled.

"Did he tell you that?" Jackson asked.

"No, not exactly. He did not come right out and say that, but it was obvious. It's been a long time coming. You're pretty observant. If you had been around him more, you would have seen it coming too," Kat answered.

"I did," Jackson responded.

"Wow! Why don't you just say I told you so and get it over with? That might be easier to swallow," Kat said.

"Sorry," Jackson replied. He kept looking over Kat's right shoulder. He was not staring; it was only an occasional glance, but he was keeping an eye on something going on behind Kat's back. It was becoming evident with each passing second that Jackson was not chasing a girl. The only person behind Kat was extremely large man. Although, with any luck at all, Jackson could be watching the waitress for that back table.

"How bad is it?" Kat asked cutting her eyes to her right side without moving her head.

"Am I that obvious?" Jackson asked.

"Nah, not really. Please tell me she's just some girl you're trying to make jealous," Kat pleaded.

"Nah, not really," Jackson reacted.

"It's that great big guy in the back corner who came in about an hour ago, isn't it?" Kat asked.

"What happened to your don't ask, don't tell approach?" Jackson asked.

"That was before I sat down between you and what I don't want to know about," Kat explained.

"What are you drinking?" Jackson asked changing the subject.

"Strawberry daiquiri," Kat answered.

"How long have you been here?" Jackson asked.

"Couple hours, maybe longer," Kat answered.

"Have you even touched that daiquiri?" Jackson asked.

"I have. Jackson, should I leave?" Kat asked.

Jackson shook his head. "You'll be fine. There's nothing to worry about besides, I hear you can handle yourself. I met Owen Grier today, who had a very interesting story to tell about you."

Kat rolled her eyes. "I can't believe he's still talking about that."

"I can't either. Listen, if I had my butt kicked by a girl, nobody would know about it. I would make sure of that," Jackson said.

"Owen was always a weird one," Kat pointed out.

"He still is," Jackson agreed. "So what's your side of the story? What happened?" Jackson inquired.

"I still can't believe I lost my cool like that. Owen always thought he was real funny, but he never thought before he spoke. I guess he was sort of the dumb jock type in a way."

"So he was a pretty big guy?" Jackson interrupted.

"I don't know. What do you consider a big guy? He played football," Kat replied.

"Man!" Jackson exclaimed. "A real jock."

"Anyway, he was giving me a hard time, trying to be funny. He was teasing me about how I didn't know my parents. I had no idea where they were, and I never hear from them. He was saying that the only reason my aunt wanted me is because she lost her baby and couldn't get pregnant again. After she couldn't have children her husband wound up leaving her. Owen was telling everyone that my aunt was the only one who wanted me and that she only wanted me because it was better than being alone. I only gave him one warning to shut up. Then I just lost it. I wasn't thinking. I just did it. Everything was kind of a blur until it was over. The next thing I remember Owen was lying on the floor covered in blood. It turns out that it all came from his nose, but I was scared to death when I saw all the blood. My aunt has never been so mad. For just over four months, I didn't do anything except eat, sleep, school, and church," Kat recalled.

"Mmm, that's awesome," Jackson said.

"Awesome? What was so awesome about it? I've never been so ashamed in my life. I never even worked up the nerve to tell my aunt why I did it," Kat admitted.

"You were in high school, right?" Jackson asked.

"Yeah, I was in tenth; Owen was in eleventh," Kat answered.

"Man, that's what is so awesome. You literally laid out a high school football player. I mean Owen isn't a small guy now; I can only imagine back when he was actually pumping iron. Owen said you were using some kind of martial arts moves," Jackson said.

"Yeah, several witnesses said that same thing, but I don't know how to do that kind of thing. I've never had any sort of lessons. My aunt didn't even let me watch any violent movies," Kat added.

"So what are you trying to say? That was all instinct?" Jackson asked.

"Yeah, I guess it would have to be," Kat answered.

"No, uh-uh, there is no way. You aren't just born knowing that stuff. Just think. You did all that stuff without even thinking. Someone had to have taught you that," Jackson said.

"Well, they didn't. No one ever taught me anything like that. I don't know how to do it again, and I don't want to do it again. Look, I can't handle myself. Should I go?" Kat asked again.

"There's no reason for you to leave unless you just can't stand sitting here with me another minute, but you're actually giving me a perfect excuse to get a lot closer than I could any other way," Jackson answered.

"Are you sure?" Kat persisted.

"Yeah, I'm positive, but it will be a lot easier for both of us if we talk about something else," Jackson advised.

"Well, OK… I heard S & R went under," Kat said awkwardly trying to make conversation.

Jackson nodded his head in agreement. "So what?"

Kat stared at Jackson a minute. "There was more to that fall than just what made the news, huh?" Kat prompted.

"What do you think?" Jackson asked refusing to bite.

"I think there was a lot more to it, maybe some corruption, and I think that you were somehow right there in the middle of it. How about that?" Kat plotted.

"Are you accusing me of corruption?" Jackson asked.

"Is that what I'm saying?… I think you know what I'm saying. Am I right?" Kat challenged.

Jackson grinned and shook his head. He leaned across the table and whispered, "Come here."

Kat leaned across the table until she was face to face with Jackson.

"I…" Jackson's eyes darted to Kat's right. "I've got to go," he said. He jumped up and quickly made his way to the front door.

The following weekend Kat was in Wal-Mart picking up a few things to get ready for the end of the school year when the same big guy from the sports bar and grill walked up to her. "Who was your friend?" he asked in a gruff voice.

"I'm sorry?" Kat said.

"Last week, the guy in the bar, who was he?" the man asked again.

"He's a friend from church. I'm sorry; do I know you?" Kat asked.

"No. Your friend is working for me this summer. What's your opinion of him? Is he a hard worker?" the man questioned.

"I guess. I really only know him from church functions," Kat answered.

The man nodded and walked off. Kat worried the rest of the afternoon and all night long. She got very little sleep that night. The next day Jackson was running late to church. Sunday School had already started when he arrived. Their Sunday School class almost always let out late. It was always a mad dash to get to the sanctuary in time for the start of the service, but Kat stopped Jackson anyway. "Can I talk to you a minute?"

Jackson looked at Kat suspiciously. "Sure, shoot," he agreed.

Kat waited until everyone else cleared out on their way to the sanctuary. "That guy from the restaurant the other day," Kat started in a real low tone.

"Whoa," Jackson interrupted. "Let's get out of here." He grabbed Kat's arm and he pulled her out to his pick up. "Get in," he told Kat. Jackson climbed in. As soon as he pulled out of the church parking lot, he started out of town. "I liked it better when you didn't want to know anything for everyone's safety. It's too late for that now, so ask me," he said.

"I don't want to ask you anything," Kat replied.

"That's just too bad. I cannot come out and tell you anything without getting into a lot of trouble, but if you put two and two together on your own and ask me about it, I can do a little damage control," Jackson explained.

"I don't want to know anything. I'm not asking," Kat proclaimed.

"You have got to ask me so that I can give you a run down of what it is safe to talk about and what's not. For both our sakes, just ask me," Jackson persisted.

"All I wanted to tell you is that the guy from the restaurant stopped me in Wal-Mart," Kat said.

"What?" Jackson reacted.

"I was in Wal-Mart yesterday, and he stopped me," Kat repeated.

"Are you sure it was the same guy?" Jackson asked.

"I'm positive. I'm not stupid; I'm pretty observant, and besides, he asked about you," Kat retorted.

Jackson gave Kat a worried look. "What did he ask you?"

"He asked who you were, and I told him you were a friend from church. He said that you were working for him this summer. He asked what kind of worker you were, if you were a hard worker. I told him that I guessed so but that I really only knew you from church functions," Kat explained.

"Is that all?" Jackson asked.

"Uh-huh," Kat answered a little preoccupied. She was busy watching the side view mirror.

"Are you sure?" Jackson asked.

"Positive. Jackson, do you recognize that black truck behind us? It's been following us since we left the church. The windows are too dark. I can't see in," Kat said.

Jackson glanced into the rear view mirror. "Oh no," he moaned.

"What?" Kat inquired.

"Speak of the devil," Jackson replied.

"No way. Are you kidding me?" Kat reacted.

"Don't panic. Just act natural like we planned to leave together and go get something to eat," Jackson instructed.

"My aunt is expecting me for lunch," Kat protested.

"Kat," Jackson said disapprovingly.

"I can call her when church lets out," Kat suggested.

"Good idea," Jackson said.

"You said that I had nothing to worry about, no reason to leave, remember? Why is that guy stopping me now in the store? Why is he following us?" Kat asked.

"I have no idea," Jackson answered.

"Yes you do," Kat insisted angrily.

"If you want answers, then you know which question to start with," Jackson pushed.

"Jackson," Kat said pleadingly.

"Kat, ask me," Jackson said calmly.

"No," Kat insisted stubbornly.

"Then I don't know what you're talking about," Jackson replied.

"Shut up, Jackson! Just shut up!" Kat snapped.

"First you want me to talk; now you want me to shut up. You need to make up your mind, Kat. You're way too fickle. Maybe this whole thing is in your head. Maybe you're paranoid," Jackson said.

"Jackson, shut up. I'm warning you," Kat said very annoyed.

"Oh, you're warning me? Kind of like you warned Owen Grier? Really, Kat, I'd love to see some of those moves that Owen was telling me about, but I don't think today is the best day for that. Could I take a rain check?" Jackson teased.

"Oh, you're real funny," Kat growled.

"I try," Jackson said with a wink. "How does bar-b-que sound?"

"Whatever," Kat responded.

"Come on, now. I was just giving you a hard time. The last thing we need at this point is for you to walk in there like you're ready to knock my head off," Jackson reasoned.

"I'm fine," Kat claimed.

"Yeah, right," Jackson said sarcastically.

"Shut up, and worry about yourself," Kat snapped back.

"You can help make this whole thing go away, or you can blow this whole thing out of proportion. Just don't say I didn't warn you," Jackson added.

Jackson pulled into a large parking lot. The parking lot was practically empty. They had easily missed the lunch crowd. The hostess seated them right away. The guy tailing them was seated in a different section but still in clear view.

"Have you ever been here before?" Jackson asked Kat. Kat shook her head no. "The food is excellent. This is the place that they talked about getting to cater the Valentine banquet," Jackson pointed out.

"Oh, really? Am I the only one who hasn't been here before?" Kat joked.

"Maybe so. Do you like bar-b-que?" Jackson asked.

"I love bar-b-que," Kat answered.

"I can't believe you've never been here before. You'll have to bring your aunt back sometime," Jackson suggested.

Kat and Jackson got quiet a minute as they read over the menu. While the waitress was taking their order, Kat kicked Jackson under the table and looked at a couple sitting sort of a diagonal behind Jackson. Jackson turned around to look at the couple. After the waitress left, Kat asked, "Do you know those people back there? They've been staring at us since they sat down."

"The guy used to work at S & R. I wouldn't worry about it if I were you. There are a lot of the guys from S & R who don't like me very much anymore," Jackson shrugged off.

"Can't say that I blame them, but why don't they like you anymore?" Kat asked.

"It's nothing really. There are rumors going around that I had inside information that S & R was about to go under, and that's why I got a construction job so quick afterwards," Jackson explained.

"Construction?" Kat pushed for more information.

"Yes, construction," Jackson repeated.

"What kind of construction?" Kat asked.

"Mostly homes and stuff, but I guess it ultimately depends on what people need built this summer… What?" Jackson asked.

"I didn't say anything," Kat protested.

"You made a face."

"I did not make a face," Kat insisted.

"I distinctly saw a face."

"You did? Are you sure? That's a pretty humanistic characteristic. Are you sure that's what you saw?" Kat asked sarcastically.

"OK, fine, smart aleck, what do you think about construction?" Jackson asked.

"I don't know. I've never really thought about it before. There's nothing wrong with construction. It's a very important job. Are you asking me what I think about construction over all or what I think about you in construction?" Kat asked.

"What's wrong with me in construction?" Jackson asked.

"There is absolutely nothing wrong with you in construction if you can cut it," Kat taunted.

"What is that supposed to mean, if I can cut it?" Jackson asked.

"Nothing, I just can't see you doing that. That's all."

"Oh, OK. Why can't you see me doing that?"

"I don't know. I guess you've worked in the courthouse. You've worked in a bank. You've worked in an office building. This is just a big change, and it will take some adjustment," Kat explained.

"So basically," but Jackson was interrupted by the waitress bringing out the food. "Good grief, Kat, did you get a big enough platter?"

"I didn't know it was this big," Kat defended.

"OK, so basically, what you're saying is that you don't think I can get down and get dirty doing manual labor," Jackson accused.

"That is not necessarily what I'm saying," Kat corrected.

"You would be amazed at all the jobs I can handle," Jackson bragged.

"OK, that's great, big shot. Can we talk about something different?" Kat asked.

"Please," Jackson responded.

For the next few minutes no one said anything.

"What's wrong with the slaw?" Jackson asked.

"Nothing, I don't like slaw," Kat answered.

"You're kidding," Jackson said as he reached across the table and started eating the slaw off Kat's plate. He was sure that would aggravate her, but amazingly enough she was OK with it. Everything about this meal was calm. This was the first civil conversation Jackson could remember having with Kat in a long time. "Do you like fried pickles?" he asked.

"Love them," Kat answered.

"Hate them," Jackson said, but Kat was already eating the fried pickles off his plate.

"Hey, Jackson, did you have inside information on S & R?" Kat asked.

Jackson rolled his eyes. "What do you think?"

"Hmm," Kat said as she popped another fried pickle into her mouth.

"Well?" Jackson pushed.

"Well what?" Kat asked.

"What do you think?" Jackson clarified.

"What does it matter what I think?"

"It doesn't," Jackson answered. "Don't forget to call your aunt."

"Thanks," Kat said and pulled a cell phone out of her pocket. "Hey, Aunt Rudy, I'm not going to make it for lunch… I know. Everything is fine. I ran into an old friend and couldn't weasel my way out of lunch… I love you too. Bye."

"That phone call was wrong on so many levels. You are such a liar," Jackson accused. She was good at it too. For Jackson to say that he was less than impressed would be a lie in itself. Her lie was believable, and considering that she was usually a trustworthy person, why would anyone not believe her? "You couldn't weasel out of lunch with an old friend?"

"What did you want me to say? I've been kidnapped, but don't worry. Yeah, right. She would be scared out of her mind," Kat said.

"Hold up. Kidnapped? I beg your pardon. Is that what you think this is?" Jackson asked.

"What would you call it?" Kat asked.

"I call it lunch," Jackson claimed.

"Yeah, OK," Kat mumbled.

"Listen, no one is holding you here. If you want to leave, then get up and walk out," Jackson prompted.

"Sure, I can walk all the way back to my car, huh," Kat responded.

"Has this become all about you?" Jackson asked.

"What?" Kat reacted stunned.

"Are you ready to go? Can we get the check?" Jackson asked the waitress as she rushed by.

The waitress came back quickly with the check. Jackson grabbed the check off the corner of the table, threw a tip down on the table, and bolted to the register to pay.

"How much do I owe you?" Kat asked as she climbed into the truck. Jackson already had the truck cranked and was ready to pull out.

"Don't worry about it. Picking up the tab is the least I can do after kidnapping you, princess," Jackson smarted off. Kat started to swing her left arm towards Jackson, but he caught her arm in mid swing. "Watch it, Jackie Chan!"

"What?" Kat reacted. She was already aggravated with Jackson; the last thing she needed was his childish teasing.

"Don't start your martial arts nonsense on me. I know I told you I'd love to see some of those moves Owen told me about, but now is still not the time," Jackson snapped.

"Whatever," Kat said. There it was, his teasing, but he was actually upset with her. This was not her fault; he had no reason to be upset with her. He was taking things out of context. She jerked her arm back and rolled her eyes. The truck got very quiet for a few minutes. "I didn't mean it the way it came out, by the way," Kat said.

"Didn't mean what?" Jackson asked.

At least he sounded calm again. "The kidnapping crack, I didn't mean it exactly the way you took it. I mean I said kidnapped, and I meant kidnapped. That's really the best way to describe it, but it's not what you would think of as a traditional kidnapping. I didn't want to go with you, but I kind of had to. You did literally pull me out to your truck; if you know a better word to describe it, I'm all ears. It wasn't a traditional kidnapping in the sense that I was never in any danger, and I knew what was going on the whole time," Kat tried to explain.

"You're not helping. Just drop it," Jackson suggested. He reached up and flipped the radio on. They were not far from the church by this point. Jackson dropped Kat off at her car, and they parted ways without another word.

At the next game night Jackson leaned down next to Kat's ear and whispered, "I need to talk to you alone before you leave tonight." Kat nodded.

As usual Kat and Jackson dominated at Clue. Afterwards they hung around in the church parking lot waiting for everyone to clear out. Finally the parking lot dwindled down to three, Kat, Jackson, and a new comer who was very fascinated with Kat and Jackson's superior Clue skills. At last the new guy called it a night and left.

"Is everything OK?" Kat asked Jackson.

"Yeah, everything is fine as far as I can tell. That guy doesn't believe that we are just friends from church. He's convinced that we are sneaking around. Even when you tried to take a swing at me on the way back, he thought we were holding hands or something. I couldn't convince him that we were friends, but you're off the hook," Jackson explained.

"That's fine. I don't care what he thinks as long as he stays away from me," Kat said. Something about that guy gave Kat the creeps. He did not seem trustworthy. He was too interested to be a simple boss, and he was bold to approach Kat in Wal-Mart the way he did. That made Kat terribly uneasy, not to mention the fact that he had been spying on them. Kat was being perfectly honest with Jackson and herself when she said that she did not care what he thought. As long as he stayed away and she was in the clear, the man could believe whatever tickled his fancy as far as Kat was concerned.

# Chapter 5

At the end of July, Kat made a trip down to Destin, Florida for an annual teaching conference. When Kat and a few of her colleagues were checking in, Kat spotted Jackson across the lobby. He shot her a funny look and sat down on a couch. He lounged back on the sofa. He looked relaxed, content to sit for a while, like he was waiting on someone.

Kat finished checking in. She told her friends she would be right back. She walked over to Jackson and sat down beside him. "What are you doing here?" she asked quietly.

"I should be asking you the same thing," Jackson said.

"There's a teaching conference down here this week. I come down every year for the conference and you?" Kat asked.

"I followed you know who," Jackson whispered very quietly.

You know who? That was how they were referring to him now? That in itself sounded a little childish or maybe like something from Harry Potter, but you know who was fine with Kat as long as she didn't have to be involved with anything to do with him. "That's just wonderful. Why can I not seem to avoid you and you know who?" Kat mumbled.

"I think your party is waiting on you," Jackson said gesturing toward the women that Kat had checked in with. They were standing in a tight huddle watching Kat with wide grins. They were whispering to one another and giggling. A group of young teachers, great, they would take a special interest in everything to do with the hot guy from Destin, and the rumor mill would fly when they got back home.

Two of the girls were practically jumping up and down by the time Kat back over to the group. "Kat, who is that deliciously yummy man you were talking to?"

"Just a guy I know from church," Kat tried to brush off.

"Just a guy from church, huh? What's he doing down here?"

"Vacation."

"And, we're supposed to believe that you are both down here at the same time by coincidence?"

"Believe what you want. I was just as surprised to see him down here as you were to see me talking to him."

Later that night, Kat ran into Jackson again. Kat and her friends walked into a restaurant to eat and found Jackson sitting alone. He motioned them to sit with him. All Kat's friends were eager to join Jackson and find out as much about him as possible, so Kat was not left with much choice. She sat down next to Jackson. "You have impeccable timing," Jackson whispered into her ear.

"Figures," Kat commented.

Jackson was quite the charmer. He was really laying it on thick. He had all Kat's friends eating out of the palm of his hand. Only Kat noticed how preoccupied Jackson was, and she did not dare look to see what or who was holding his attention. Kat was under the assumption that she had shaken the guy from the sports bar and grill; the last thing she wanted right now was to turn around and see him again. Of course that's who she would find if she turned around. What else would have brought Jackson all the way to Destin, Florida? Why was Jackson following this guy first to a sports bar and now to another state? No! Kat refused to think about the crazy whys. She did not want to know.

The next afternoon, Kat had just got back to the hotel when she heard a knock at the door. Kat looked through the peep hole and saw Jackson. She opened the door. Jackson came in with a big grin on his face and shut the door behind him.

"You've got to hear what you know who thinks now. It has got to be the most ridiculous thing I've ever heard," Jackson said.

Kat rolled her eyes. "Now what?"

"He thinks I followed you down here instead of him. He thinks things are getting serious between us and that we must be getting married soon. I just kept quiet and let the guy think whatever far fetched story he could come up with. I mean come on. How did he even get to that scenario? Some people should really get their assuming in check," Jackson retold.

"Are you serious?" Kat asked, but Jackson was too busy laughing to respond. He was holding his side as if he was in actual pain, and he was slightly hunched over. He was laughing too hard to even stand up straight. He genuinely looked like he might fall to the floor laughing at any given second.

Kat got so tickled at Jackson's endless laughter that she started to laugh. "Jackson, get out of here," she laughed and opened the door. She could hear Jackson laughing all the way down the hall.

Kat's first Sunday back home, she was approached right off the bat by one of the other singles. "Congratulations on your engagement. I just heard," she said.

"What!?" Kat reacted in confusion.

"Oh, no! Were you trying to keep it quiet for now? Well, the cat's out of the bag. We all know about your engagement to Jackson," the lady said.

"Oh… um…" Kat started, but she never got the chance to respond. The lady was off and running.

Jackson did not make it to Sunday School. All morning long, one person after another came up to Kat to congratulate her. Jackson barely made it before the service started.

"Oh, right here, Jackson. We can move over," Aunt Rudy's friend called after Jackson.

Everyone moved over and wedged Jackson into a full pew right next to Kat. Jackson leaned next to Kat's ear. "What's going on?"

"Eleven people have approached me already this morning to congratulate me on our engagement. Maybe you can tell me what's going on," Kat whispered.

"What? What did you tell them?" Jackson asked.

"What do you think I told them? I was in shock. All I said was oh. Then they left before I could say anything else," Kat whispered.

"Kat, that's not funny," Jackson whispered.

"No, it's not, genius. How did this happen?" Kat asked.

"I have no idea. Can we talk about this after church?" Jackson asked.

"Oh, you can bet on it," Kat whispered.

Before the preacher started his sermon, he congratulated Kat and Jackson in front of the entire congregation. If looks could kill, Jackson would have killed over dead at that very moment. The look that Kat was shooting his way was enough to take down even the toughest opponent. Jackson shrugged his shoulders and turned his head away from Kat.

Kat and Jackson left church together after they eventually got away from everyone's congratulations.

"OK, what have you done, and how are you going to fix it?" Kat snapped after they got into Jackson's truck.

"Me? What makes you think I did this? I was late today. For all I know, you started the rumor yourself this morning," Jackson returned.

"You have some nerve! Jackson, what is happening?" Kat asked. He really was an arrogant man, but could he really be this full of himself?

"I don't know, Kat. I'm as confused as you are. Granted I didn't correct you know who, but he was the only one. It had to come from him," Jackson reasoned.

"Fine, now we know where it came from. How are we going to fix it?" Kat asked.

"I don't know. He obviously knows someone at church and talks to them quite often. Who knows? Someone at church may be working with you know who," Jackson said.

"What do you mean working with him? You work with him," Kat interjected.

That was more than Jackson meant to let slip. He silently cursed himself for being so careless. "Point is if we tell the church the truth, I have to tell you know who the truth also," Jackson continued.

"Then what happens?" Kat asked desperately.

"That's just it. I don't know what might happen," Jackson admitted.

"So what do we do?" Kat asked solemnly.

"I don't know. What can we do? We'll just have to go along with the lie until I can figure out who all is involved with this mess," Jackson decided.

"Are you serious?" Kat asked in disbelief. The nerve of this guy! What did he think he was doing, and who did he think gave him the authority to do that?

"I guess so; do you have a better idea?" Jackson asked.

"How long do you think it will take?" Kat inquired. Why was she even asking that? She couldn't seriously be thinking of going along with this insanity, could she?

"I have no clue. Would you just lay off? This was really unexpected. Try to be patient," Jackson said.

Jackson had obviously been blind sighted with this as genuinely as Kat. Kat still believed that Jackson's intentions were good, and you-know-who still gave her the creeps. How long could it possibly take Jackson to get this whole thing sorted out? He was a smart guy and resourceful. What would it hurt to play along for a little while? There it was; she was caving in. She was going to play along with this deluded fantasy. As much as she hated this whole situation, something still gave her an eerie feeling that outweighed her annoyance.

"OK," Kat agreed.

That afternoon Kat was approached by Aunt Rudy. "So, you're engaged?" Aunt Rudy demanded. It really was more of an accusation than a question. Aunt Rudy's stance was defensive and stiff. Her eyebrows were pulled together trying desperately to hide the pain that was painted all over her face. Kat hated seeing her aunt hurt, especially knowing that she was the one who had put the hurt there. Aunt Rudy was the only one Kat had; Kat was as protective of Aunt Rudy as Aunt Rudy was of her. That was another reason why Kat was going along with Jackson.

Kat did not know what Jackson was involved in. Sure, she didn't want to know, but that also meant that she didn't know how much danger was involved or how wide spread that danger would be. Kat could never forgive herself if she thought she put Aunt Rudy in danger, danger that could have been prevented by something as simple as letting people believe that she was engaged to Jackson.

"That's what the talk is," Kat said nonchalantly hoping to blow it off without further hurt feelings.

"Why did I have to hear it from the grapevine instead of straight from you?"

Kat pulled in a deep breath. She wasn't sure how much danger telling the truth could get her into. She wasn't about to put her aunt in possible danger. She hated lying to her aunt, but it wasn't something that could be helped this time. "Aunt Rudy, it wasn't something that we put a lot of planning into. It just sort of happened. We hadn't meant to tell anyone. We don't have any idea how it got out."

"That isn't the point, Kat. I didn't even know the two of you were dating."

"We weren't," Kat responded too soon. "I mean we were friends, but… It all just happened so fast. Please don't be mad. Of course I wanted to tell you first. I just can't understand what happened."

"I'm not mad, Kat… I'm just… I don't know."

Hurt, Kat thought. That was exactly what her aunt was not saying. She was hurt.

Kat pulled into the church parking lot right behind Jackson Wednesday night. "Well, are you ready to do this?" Jackson asked Kat.

"Nope, not at all. Let's go," Kat admitted.

Other church members wasted no time. Kat and Jackson were practically mowed down at the door. Everyone wanted to hug their neck. That's what Southern Baptist do; they hug. They hug to greet. They hug to console, and they hug to congratulate. Kat and Jackson were immediately swallowed up in a sea of emotion.

"There they are. Aren't they cute together," one lady said.

Another lady asked, "When is the wedding?"

"Oh well, we haven't really picked a date yet," Jackson jumped in.

"You need to go ahead and get your wedding on the calendar as soon as possible," the preacher suggested.

"What's the hold up?" Mrs. Judy asked. "What are you still discussing? Kat wants to get married on January first. I remember her telling me that. She said that when she gets married, that's the way she wants to start the year from day one. That was an important point with her. Are you seriously making her change that?"

"Of course not," Jackson reacted taken off guard.

"Great, I just don't see enough winter weddings," the preacher commented.

"January first, oh, I'm so excited," another lady chimed in.

"This January?" Kat asked.

Kat was not sure what to say. She was not expecting to pick a date. She never dreamed it would go that far. Now she was seriously regretting ever agreeing to go along with this cockamamie scheme. What was any of this to her? It certainly wasn't her problem. How could any of it come back on her if she didn't play along? Then again that unnamed guy had approached her at Wal-Mart. Maybe he would make sure that it would come back on her. Was he dangerous? There was definitely something about him that did not sit well with Kat. Would he be a threat to her? Would he be a threat to the people she loved? What had Jackson gotten her into?

"Surely you don't want to wait another year and a half. Do you?" Aunt Rudy asked. She gave Kat an almost challenging look.

"Of course not, Rudy, don't be ridiculous," Mrs. Judy added.

Had that really just happened? Had they really set a date without any help whatsoever from Kat? Kat was too stunned to say anything or interject a single word. She tried to focus as the two ladies began discussing everything that would have to be done.

# Chapter 6

Week by week every detail of the wedding was planned out in very much the same way. Kat and Jackson said very little, but somehow a picture perfect wedding was planned out around them. Like most grooms Jackson steered clear of any and all wedding plans, and Kat did not know what to say. She walked around in a daze, as if she was watching everything from a distance. She watched everything unfold as everyone but she planned a wedding.

Since Kat did not have too much to say everyone simply assumed what she wanted and pulled her along. They took the slightest movement or even a strange look to be the answer they so desired. In fact, everyone was so excited over the whole ordeal that no one even noticed that Kat had been excluded. Everything was severely out of control. A whole wedding was being planned, and Kat was still too stunned to speak. Her mind was full and constantly swirling with worry and questions.

What was going on? How long was this going to go on? What was taking Jackson so long? Why had he not fixed it yet? How hard could it be? How far was this going to go? Kat knew she needed to stop it. When did she need to stop it? How much more time could she possibly give Jackson?

By November almost everything was planned and set in place, even the smallest details. Aunt Rudy invited Jackson to spend Thanksgiving with them. Neither Kat nor Jackson had much to say.

"This is getting way out of hand," Kat told Jackson the very first chance they got alone.

"No joke," Jackson agreed.

"I'm serious. Do you realize that bride's maids have been asked and dresses have been chosen?" Kat pointed out.

"Already?" Jackson asked in disbelief.

"Yes, they've already started alterations on the wedding dress," Kat confirmed. "The so called wedding is in less than two months. Of course they have the dresses. Alterations on my dress are all that's left for the dresses."

"Wow!" Jackson mumbled.

"Exactly, so what's up? Are you close to getting a handle on this situation?" Kat asked.

"I'm making progress," Jackson said.

Kat took a deep breath, and they rejoined Aunt Rudy. It was easy to take that as the answer she wanted. Everyone else could stretch answers to meet their desires; so could she.

Kat noticed that Jackson looked worried. Maybe she was not the only one stressed over everything going on. Kat had been in such a stunned state of panic that she had not stopped to think about this from Jackson's point of view. It had to be dreadful on his side as well. It was probably worse. He had a lot more to think about. He could not afford the same distraction Kat could, so she decided that she could give him a couple more weeks, but somehow Kat seemed to miss the time slipping by.

December seemed to fly by. Kat and Jackson did not talk much to anyone including each other. Kat was flustered and did not want to talk to anyone about anything. With so many wheels in motion, how could she ever stop them now? So much money had already been spent. Kat would never see that money again. At least she had saved back a little nest egg for a rainy day. That was the only comfort. She never would have forgiven herself if she knew she was costing Aunt Rudy all that money for nothing.

Jackson wasn't talking much either. He was reclusive, holding back, and Kat began to see something in Jackson that she had never seen before. She saw fear. She had never known Jackson to ever show fear. Kat was more than a little frightened; she was terrified at this new development. How bad did things have to get before Jackson showed fear? How many people were in danger? Would people die? How could she stop playing along now? What would be the consequences?

Christmas was every bit as awkward as Thanksgiving had been. Dinner at Aunt Rudy's was quite the event. Aunt Rudy and Kat cooked all morning long and set a beautiful table. There was enough food to feed a small army.

"Jackson, don't take this the wrong way. I'm thrilled that you are spending Christmas with us, but don't you have family that you usually spend Christmas with. I mean, I did have y'all for Thanksgiving. It hardly seems fair," Aunt Rudy said.

"Oh… ah, too far. We are all spread out across the country, sometimes outside the country. We can't always get together for holidays… Everything looks delicious."

"I hope you're hungry," Aunt Rudy said.

Everyone ate too much. After lunch Kat insisted that Aunt Rudy go sit down to rest and let her clean up the kitchen. "I'll get the dishes. You've done so much getting ready for today. Let me do this. You go sit down for a while; I know you're exhausted."

"There's too much for one person to tackle alone," Aunt Rudy protested.

"I'll give her a hand. She's right; you deserve a break. Go on. This is our way of saying thank you," Jackson added. It is weird the way some things catch your attention. Our way, Jackson though. They were a we now somehow. They had gone from barely tolerating each other to an odd sort of team. This whole mess had bonded them in a way that could never be undone.

Aunt Rudy gave in reluctantly and went to the living room to stretch out in her recliner a minute.

"How is it going?" Kat asked once they were safely tucked away alone in the kitchen.

"Fine. How's everything going with you?"

"That's not exactly what I meant."

"Kat, I know what you meant. I'm making progress."

"That's what you said last month."

"It's still true."

"OK… promise?"

"Yes, Kat!"

"Don't get mad at me! I just want to know that you are doing everything possible. I don't want to do this."

"You think I do!? Look, I'm taking care of it."

"Fine, that's all I wanted to know."

Just like always time continued to pass, and it seems like you blink your eyes after Christmas and New Year's is here. Soon the big day was here, and nothing had been settled. Kat and Jackson actually went through with the wedding.

What other choice was there? Surely Jackson would back out if there was any other choice. His face overflowed with fear. Could no one else see the fear that Kat saw? What would happen if Kat bailed now? She obviously had no choice, so Kat continued to play the role she had been assigned.

Kat shot Jackson funny looks throughout the entire ceremony. Jackson's gaze darted franticly around the sanctuary throughout the entire ceremony. It was like he was looking for someone. Was Jackson expecting family? Kat didn't remember him mentioning anything about his family.

Kat followed the preacher's lead blindly. She listened numbly as Jackson did the same. He slid a ring on her hand. The ring looked ominous. That tiny little circle represented a lot, and this time it represented more than anyone guessed. Kat slid a ring on Jackson's hand. It was the most physical contact she had ever had with him. He had thick, masculine hands that were noticeably strong. Kat had not noticed before just how strong Jackson was. Long muscles rippled up and down the length of his hands as he moved and continued up his arms. Jackson was absolutely as strong physically as he was mentally. So, why had someone so strong in every way not been able to get them out of this situation?

It was done. Vows had been made, and now the preacher was saying, "I now pronounce you man and wife. You may kiss the bride." Jackson leaned in close and pressed his lips gently to hers with a soft pressure. His lips were soft, warm… nice. His tongue swept swiftly over her lips. His tongue barely grazed her, and then he was gone. It was short but… sweet. It was sad to admit, but that had been the best kiss Kat had in years.

"I'm honored to introduce to you, for the very first time, Mr. and Mrs. Jackson Johnson."

No one who saw Kat or Jackson during the reception would have ever guessed that the smiles on their faces were fake. If that could even genuinely be called a smile. What she saw on Jackson's face was more of a grimace, and she felt sure that his was a mirror of her own face.

After the reception Kat and Jackson were on their way to Gatlinburg. Mr. Carter, a member of the church, owned a cabin in Gatlinburg and offered it to Kat and Jackson for their honeymoon. There was a huge turn out to see Kat and Jackson off. They created a path from the churches front doors right up to the truck. Bubbles floated all around them, and everyone was cheering. It was all very surreal.

"I think I'm going to throw up," Kat mumbled after they had been on the road a little less than a half hour.

"Are you OK?" Jackson asked.

"Am I OK?" Kat repeated. "Of course I'm not OK. We just got married."

"Calm down. I'm making progress," Jackson said.

"Progress? That's what you said at Thanksgiving and again at Christmas," Kat reminded him. She tried to remain calm, but she was failing miserably. She was all but yelling at Jackson now despite the unease in her stomach.

"I know. It's a slow process, but I am making progress. Give me time. I'll put everything back together," Jackson said.

"You'll put everything back together. How do you purpose to do that? It's done now, and it can't be undone. I don't believe in divorce. Well, I do. I believe people get divorces, but it's more like a separation. If you get a divorce then get remarried, you're living a life of adultery. A marriage is a binding union from God. What does man made law have to do with it at that point?" Kat explained.

"That's great, Kat. Mentioning your thoughts on the subject a little earlier might would have helped. Even as late as this morning would have made a difference," Jackson said.

"Oh, I'm going to be sick," Kat mumbled.

"Well, what do you want me to do about it now?" Jackson snapped. "Wait a minute. What about Kelley White? He was divorced and you dated him."

"I made a mistake, and I learned from it. I won't make that mistake again," Kat answered.

The ride got very quiet for a long time; in fact, they made it all the way to the cabin before either of them spoke again. It was a nice cabin, secluded in the woods with no one around to intrude on a newlywed couple's privacy. There was a hot tub on the back porch and the promise of more romantic luxury inside. Kat and Jackson didn't need any of it. Not the privacy, not the hot tub, not the romantic luxury, they were not a real couple, and this was a lousy marriage doomed from the beginning.

"I didn't realize that you and Mr. Carter were this close," Kat mentioned as they carried suitcases inside.

"We aren't. I thought you were close," Jackson replied.

"Not even, Mr. Carter has never liked me," Kat corrected.

Kat and Jackson stopped dead in their tracks and looked at each other.

"We've got to get back!" Jackson said hastily, and they both turned around and ran back to the truck.

They had not been back on the road ten minutes yet when Kat said, "Oh, wait. It couldn't have been Mr. Carter. He was in the middle of a month long mission trip when this whole mess got started."

Jackson spun the truck back around and grumbled, "Perfect," as Kat grasped the door in one hand and the console in the other.

"What was that about?" Kat snapped. Jackson did not answer assuming that she meant his reckless driving. "You have no idea yet. I thought you said you were making progress," Kat accused.

"I am making progress. I told you this is a slow process," Jackson defended.

"What process it that? What exactly are you doing?" Kat asked.

"I thought you didn't want to know," Jackson reminded her.

"Yeah, well, I just changed my mind. Come on, Jackson. I'm asking. Who are you? What do you do? How are you handling this?" Kat shouted.

"Are you sure about that?" Jackson asked.

"Positive," Kat growled.

"OK, I work for the CIA. Almost three years ago there was an attack on the president by a terrorist sympathizer. The man was caught. Now there is a movement to flush out everyone associated with the attack and to tighten the leash on other terrorist sympathizers," Jackson explained.

"So are you flushing someone out or tightening a leash?" Kat asked.

"I'm flushing out a suspect," Jackson answered.

"And you think that the guy from the bar has something to do with the attack?" Kat asked.

"I know the guy from the sports bar had something to do with the attack. I just haven't found the proof I need yet," Jackson answered.

"Does he have any affiliation with the church?" Kat asked.

"None at all," Jackson admitted, "but he obviously has connection with someone who is affiliated."

"You don't know who?" Kat asked.

"No," Jackson answered shortly.

"It's not an open connection, so it's more secretive than anything else?… Do you think the person affiliated with the church is in on it?" Kat asked.

"I don't know whether or not they were involved with the attack, but I have no reason to believe that they are not a terrorist sympathizer," Jackson replied.

Kat and Jackson both got quiet again. When they got back to the cabin, they carried their luggage in and found opposite ends of the cabin.

Late that night, Kat found Jackson asleep on a couch. "Hey, can I borrow your keys?" Kat asked gently.

"Nope," Jackson answered clearly. He had spent years putting minor adjustments here and there on his truck. Kat didn't need to be driving it and accidentally stumble upon one of his adjustments. "Why do you want my keys?"

"I'm hungry, and your truck is the only vehicle here," Kat explained.

"Hold up. I'm coming," Jackson mumbled.

"Are you serious? You would rather wake up and take me to get something to eat than let me drive your truck?" Kat questioned.

"I would rather drive asleep than hand over the keys to my truck," Jackson owned up to.

"That is ridiculous," Kat declared.

"It's not just you. I won't give my keys to anyone," Jackson admitted.

"We're at least twenty-five minutes away from anything," Kat pointed out.

"And I would rather drive you to go get something, thank you," Jackson added.

"OK, whatever floats your boat," Kat relented.

No one said anything for almost half the trip into town. Kat kept a close eye on Jackson to be sure that he did not fall to sleep behind the wheel.

"Do you think they did it on purpose?" Kat asked.

"Who did what on purpose?" Jackson reacted confused.

"The person from church in contact with the guy from the sports bar, do you think that they started the rumors on purpose? Maybe it's someone who knows us and knows we don't get along, so when the guy told them that he thought we were sneaking around, they started the rumors out of spite simply because they knew it wasn't true." Kat inquired.

"It is entirely possible," Jackson agreed, "but we must have really thrown them when we actually went through with it. It could have been that when my guy told the person from the church that we were sneaking around together, they believed him. They may have thought that our constant bickering was facade, or it could be as simple as they don't know us all that well. Maybe they know who we are; they know we are both members of the singles group, and that's all they really knew. When my guy told them that we were sneaking around together, it wasn't very hard to believe, and when my guy told them we were engaged, there was no reason why not," Jackson imagined.

"Wow… Do you have to call him your guy?" Kat asked.

"That's what he is; he's my suspect," Jackson answered.

"Calling him your guy makes it sound like you're in on it, like he works for you, or that you and he are dating. Can't you call him something else?" Kat asked.

"Like what?" Jackson responded.

"Give him a name or something. We could call him John Doe," Kat suggested.

"John Doe? OK, that's fine. You've attended that church a long time."

"As long as I can remember," Kat interrupted.

"Yeah, do you know of anyone who might be a terrorist sympathizer?" Jackson questioned.

"Yeah right. Anyone in the church who sides with Muslims, or radical anything, is not going to admit to it," Kat pointed out with scorn.

"Of course not, but you're a very observant person. Haven't you ever noticed anyone acting a little strange?" Jackson asked.

"At that church, there are a lot of people who act a little strange, but sympathizing with terrorist, I don't think so," Kat answered.

"Well, it was a nice try anyway. You can help me though, by keeping your eyes open," Jackson charged.

"No problem," Kat agreed.

## Chapter 7

For the most part Kat and Jackson kept their distance for the remainder of the so called honeymoon. When they got home, they moved into a teeny tiny apartment on a temporary basis. Jumping around from job to job, had not provided Jackson with much more income than to survive on, and Kat had spent all the money she had put back. When it was all said and done, they did not have much money to live off of. Most of their furniture had to go into storage. Very, very little would fit into the diminutive apartment. They could barely fit one bed into the small apartment. Not even a couch could squeeze into the living room. As a result they wound up with no choice but to share a bed. The bed was crammed into a corner of the bedroom, and it took up most of the space in the small bedroom. Jackson slept by the wall. Kat slept on the edge so that she had easy access to the alarm clock. Both Kat and Jackson kept to opposite sides of the bed to avoid any and all physical contact but for very different reasons.

Kat's reasoning was basic contempt. She wanted to have as little to do with Jackson as was possible in their extremely abnormal relationship. He was handsome enough, strong, and a decent guy. Maybe if things had been different, Kat could have fallen for someone like Jackson. He actually would have made someone a good catch. Even Kat could admit that, but for her things were different. This never should have happened. Although Kat knew, somewhere in the back of her mind, that she had her own share of the blame to bare, she still blamed Jackson for this whole thing. She was determinedly still mad at him, and stubborn enough to hang onto that anger. All she wanted now was to keep as much space between them as possible in their prison cell of an apartment.

Jackson, on the other hand, couldn't stand to be that close to Kat without craving more. He was male, for Pete's sake! Kat was attractive. Her beautiful body was soft and warm, and it didn't help that Jackson could not seem to get their wedding kiss off his mind. She had tasted so good, and anytime he got too close, all he wanted was to have another taste. All this played havoc on his emotions; logically Jackson knew he didn't want to be with Kat, but physically his hormones had other ideas.

"This apartment is too cramped!" Kat exclaimed.

"No joke," Jackson said sarcastically. "What do you want me to do about it?"

The truth of the matter was that Jackson could have easily rectified their living arrangements. He made plenty of money working for the CIA, but that would blow his cover out of the water. He was supposed to be somewhat of a nomad, wandering from one job to another. Suddenly coming into money would look very suspicious. Jackson did not like living in such close quarters with Kat any more than she did, but it had to be done.

"We've got to get out of here. I can't hack this much longer. Cooking in that closet is all but impossible. We can't keep eating out. We just can't afford it. I have to wait for you to go to bed first at night. If I didn't you would have to climb over me to get into bed. That is getting harder everyday. You stay up a lot later than I'm use to. All day long at school, I am absolutely give out; I'm exhausted. If we switch sides, then I would have to climb over you in the mornings, because I have to get up so much earlier than you. There is no room to move in that shower. Getting dressed in that bathroom is a joke. I have to dig through your shaving stuff everyday searching for my makeup. I can't find anywhere in here to sit down to get some grading done, and I'm already behind after that useless trip to Tennessee. There's not even room to just stop and breathe. I hate this place. I'm suffocating. We've got to get out of here ASAP!" Kat puffed.

"I agree. It's impossible to think around here. There's no where to go to get away from each other, but where else can we go? You mentioned money. If you can find something we can afford, then, please, be my guest," Jackson replied.

"I can? Are you sure?" Kat asked.

"I would love nothing more than to get out of this dinky cage, but I do not have the time to look right now," Jackson explained.

"So if I start looking, you won't get mad?" Kat checked again.

"Nope, I hope you do look, and I hope you find something. I wouldn't get my hopes up if I were you, but if you have time, please, look," Jackson replied.

"I can find time," Kat declared.

"If you don't have time, don't worry about it. You don't need to stress yourself out over it. I'll get around to it eventually," Jackson said.

"This is stressing me out," Kat said stretching her arms out to her sides. "No, believe me. I have no problem making time to find something bigger."

It took Kat less than a month to find a small place within their budget.

"I love James Bond," Kat said as she squeezed into the apartment with Jackson who was sitting on the love seat, the only piece of furniture they could fit in the apartment living room aside from the TV, watching a James Bond movie. "I love them all, really. I can't pick a favorite, but as a whole the James Bond movies are my all time favorites." Jackson did not say a word. He made no response at all. He seemed not to even acknowledge Kat. He was either completely consumed by the movie, or he was lost deep in his own thought. Either way, it did not matter. Kat was not the least bit deterred; she simply continued talking. "What are you doing this weekend?"

"I'm working. Why?" Jackson replied.

"I found a place we can afford. I want you to go with me this weekend to see it," Kat answered.

"I thought you were going to handle this. Whatever you think will be fine," Jackson said.

"Well, I haven't seen it yet, but the realtor I talked to said it was a fixer-up. That's why I would really like you to go with me. Could you take off only a couple hours Saturday? It won't take long. All you would need to do is take a look at the house and see if it's worth it or if it's a money pit," Kat responded.

"Yeah, could we do it around lunch? I can use my lunch hour; that way I only have to get off an hour," Jackson asked.

"Of course, we can do it any time you want. I'll call the realtor during my prep tomorrow and get it set up," Kat answered.

The house was small but still considerably larger than the apartment. The house was a cream color underneath all the dirt. The siding needed rinsing off, nothing too hard; a garden hose would easily do the trick. The quaint little yard needed mowing and was in desperate need of some attention. For the most part, the house was not necessarily in real bad shape. Mostly, it had just been neglected.

There was one bedroom with a full bath, a kitchen, a living room, a half-bath, and a carport with room for two cars around the back of the house. The majority of the rooms needed fresh paint. The front door opened into the living room. The living room would sooner or later need new carpeting. The carport needed some serious scrubbing, but the house did have a working dishwasher. There was a working washer and dryer in what looked like a closet. The bedroom had a couple holes in the walls that needed to be filled. One hole was the size of a baseball; the other was the size of a large cantaloupe.

The half-bath was by far in the worst shape. It needed some serious work. The mirror on the medicine cabinet was shattered. The toilet was nasty to say the least. The sink would have to be replaced. The floor was in terrible shape. It would definitely have to be re tiled if there was no worse damage underneath the old tile.

Jackson walked silently through the house, showing no emotion. Kat let the realtor do most of the talking. Kat studied Jackson's face and every move for some type of reaction.

"So what do you think?" the realtor asked hopefully.

"Can we have a minute to talk?" Jackson asked the realtor as he pointed at Kat.

"Oh of course, take all the time you need," the realtor replied.

Jackson grabbed Kat's arm and pulled her off to the side.

"What do you think?" Kat asked.

"Well, the only major damage is in the half-bath. It is going to take some time and money, but it can be closed off until I get it finished. Other than that, it really isn't that bad. What do you think?" Jackson replied.

"I think it's kind of cute. It will take a lot of effort, but it can be fixed up," Kat answered.

"OK, I've got to get back. Whatever you decide will be fine," Jackson said.

Jackson got back to the apartment just before dark that night. "Well, what did you decide?" he asked.

"We can start moving in next weekend. I talked to the landlord here. We'll have to pay for two more months, but he'll let us out of the lease. After we get the two months here paid for, we will actually be paying less a month than we are here," Kat answered.

"Great," was all that Jackson said. "Let me talk to the landlord. The lease I signed was month by month. We shouldn't have to pay for any month that we aren't living here," he added a few minutes later.

"That would be wonderful. How did you sign a month by month lease? Who offers that?" Kat asked.

"I never said he offered it. I guess it's a habit not to get into a living situation too permanent," Jackson replied.

"I guess you do move around a lot," Kat commented.

"Yeah, it has a tendency to come along with the territory," Jackson said.

That night Jackson did not go to bed until almost midnight. Kat waited until Jackson went to bed first so that he wouldn't have to climb over her. She would not have waited up for him except it made her very uncomfortable when Jackson had to climb over her. The close contact was weirdly unnerving. The longer they lived in such close quarters, the more aware Kat became of Jackson physically. There was never any doubt that he was good looking and built like a rock, but night after night he slept next to her wearing nothing but boxers. Kat had never been so tempted in her life, but she was strong willed. She could handle this. It was just raging hormones; she would work her way through it, and it would pass.

Kat was beat when Jackson finally went to bed, but although Kat was dead tired, she would not get a restful night's sleep.

Only a short two hours later, Kat's body started to shake violently from side to side. She began to whine and cry out. "No, no, you can't take me away. It's too late. Noooo! Noooooo! I can't leave. You can't make me. Noooo! You don't understand. How can you do this? Noooo! Noooooo! Nooooo!"

"Kat?" Jackson called. He held her arm, applying gentle pressure and started to shake her slightly, trying to wake her. "Kat… Kat, wake up. Kat, you're having a nightmare. Wake up."

Kat sat straight up with a jerk. She was out of breath and gasping for air. "What?" she squealed.

"You were having a nightmare," Jackson informed her.

"Really?" Kat reacted in disbelief.

"Yeah, you were moaning and groaning something about somebody couldn't take you somewhere. I don't know. You were jerking around a lot too. It's a wonder you didn't fall in the floor," Jackson explained.

"That's weird," Kat mumbled.

Jackson rolled over to his other side and was asleep in a matter of seconds.

Over the next week, Kat and Jackson got everything packed up when they got home from work. By Friday everything was ready to be moved. The plan was to get up early Saturday morning and start moving everything from the apartment to the house.

Friday night just after one-thirty, Kat started having another nightmare. She began jerking from side to side and crying out. "No! No, you can't do this. It isn't fair. Nooooooo! You can't take me away. Nooooooo!"

Jackson reached over and started shaking Kat. "Wake up. Kat, you're having another nightmare," he called.

Kat woke up with a sudden deep gasp.

"Are you OK?" Jackson asked.

"I'm fine," Kat answered breathlessly.

Jackson rolled over and went right back to sleep, but Kat could not seem to get back to sleep. All of the sudden, she had an excessive amount of nervous energy, so instead she got up and started quietly loading up her car and Jackson's truck.

Jackson did not wake up until nearly six Saturday morning. Kat had both vehicles completely loaded by that time. She had loaded everything that could be lifted by one person alone. The only things left for the second trip were things that would take both of them to lift and of course the bed which would have to be taken apart. Even though that was admittedly not the way that Jackson had intended to start, he remained calm and went with the flow.

The entire move wound up taking three trips. Everything was moved by noon, but Kat and Jackson were already exhausted and had not unpacked the first box or even reassembled the bed.

"How about we go get some lunch and take a break before we start unpacking?" Jackson suggested.

"Perfect idea," Kat agreed.

Kat and Jackson went to Wendy's. They were looking to get food fast and sit down for a while.

"I'm so tired," Jackson complained as they sat down.

"Me too," Kat agreed.

"Did you ever go back to sleep last night?" Jackson asked.

"Nah," Kat shook her head.

"What were you dreaming about? That nightmare was intense," Jackson inquired.

"Beats me. I don't remember anything but you waking me up," Kat told him.

"Wow! Last night was the same as the other night, whatever you were dreaming about. It was wild. I can't describe the way you sounded. It was too varied, like a wide range of emotions. You sounded upset, scared, and furious all at the same time. You were jerking around something terrible. If I thought you had a history of seizures, I would have called nine-one-one the first time. You don't remember anything?" Jackson asked.

"Nope, nothing. I woke up in this really awful cold sweat both nights. I was mad. I don't know why I was so mad, but I was so mad I could cry. Have you ever been that mad and had no clue who you were mad at or why? It is a dreadful feeling. Last night I couldn't go back to sleep. I had too much nervous energy," Kat described.

"What were you so nervous about?" Jackson asked.

"I don't know. I was jumpy and could not stop moving. I was extremely over active. I don't know why; I just could not calm down," Kat explained.

It was almost two by the time Kat and Jackson got back to the house. They started unpacking and worked straight on until eight o'clock. At eight, they both quit and went right to bed. There was more room now. No one had to climb over anyone to get in or out of bed. That would make things a lot more comfortable for both of them, even if they didn't have a second bed… yet. Believe it or not Kat did not mind sleeping next to Jackson as much now. Actually it was sort of a safe feeling to know he was right beside her. Jackson could be truly annoying sometimes, but Kat did feel safe around him. He could even be an OK guy from time to time.

The following day at church, Kat and Jackson moving into a new house was the hot gossip. Their house was all anyone wanted to talk about before and after both their Sunday School lesson and the service. Kat and Jackson were so tired from moving and unpacking that the house was the last thing they wanted to talk about. When they returned to church that night, their house was still the topic of choice. Sunday ended up a long day to have to endure.

Kat and Jackson continued to work at night to finish unpacking. After working all day and unpacking all evening, Kat and Jackson were asleep each night as soon as their head hit the pillow, but Wednesday night sleep was interrupted by yet another nightmare.

Kat started jerking around, crying, and screaming. Jackson started to reach over to wake Kat, but he saw Kat tumble off the side of the bed instead.

"Hey!" he shouted. He grabbed Kat and pulled her back onto the bed. "Are you OK?" Jackson asked as Kat panted heavily.

Kat nodded and said, "Thank you."

"Yeah," Jackson said and lay down to go back to sleep.

He took everything in stride. Kat wished she could maintain a constant calm like Jackson did. He rarely got worked up, and even then it was only when arguing with her. He could handle a crisis with ease. She had almost fallen off the bed for crying out loud, and Jackson simply rolled over and went back to sleep.

Over the next month, Kat had the same nightmare several more times. Jackson got to the point where he would not even wake Kat anymore. He would throw his arm over her waist to keep her from falling off the bed. Then he would either try to sleep through the nightmare or wait it out. Most nights the nightmare would not last more than twenty to thirty minutes. It was always the same, and Kat could never remember anything. It became such a natural move for Jackson to throw his arm over Kat at the slightest sound or first movement that he did not even think about it. It even became easier with time to sleep through her cries. Kat would ease out from under Jackson's arm in the morning very easily, being very careful not to wake him.

"Jackson, let me go!" Kat woke up one morning.

"What are you talking ab… Oh my goodness," Jackson reacted as he realized what was going on. Kat had another nightmare the night before. Jackson must have missed her waist when he threw his arm over her, because his arm was lying across Kat's breasts when he awoke.

"I'm sorry," Jackson apologized as he pulled his arm back. "I wasn't awake good. I… I… It wasn't on purpose." Not that he wouldn't do it on purpose if given half a chance but never without her permission.

"I didn't think it was," Kat sat up and started toward the bathroom. "I guess it beats falling in the floor," she added as she disappeared behind the bathroom door. Boy, oh, boy, did it beat falling in the floor. Jackson's big, strong, protective hand had fit around her breast as perfectly as his arm had fit around her waist. Kat leaned against the door. What was wrong with her? She was not some hormone driven teenager. She needed to get control of herself.

Throughout the next two weeks it became a regular occurrence for Jackson to wake up with his arm draped over Kat's breasts or his hand to be cupped around them after one of Kat's nightmares. Kat tried to act calm and nonchalant, but her agitation became more transparent with each occurrence. If she would admit it to herself, it wasn't the fact that he was innocuously feeling her up; it was the fact that she enjoyed it so much.

"This is getting out of hand," Jackson announced.

"Oh quite the contrary, you had more than enough in your hand this morning," Kat snarled back. Kat was past the point of mild attraction, and it was making her mad and moody.

"Exactly, I'm not doing this on purpose at all; I promise. That's why something is going to have to be done. I'm going to start sleeping on the couch until I can figure out something else," Jackson said.

Kat opened her mouth to say something, but Jackson did not give her the chance. "Don't say anything. Make sure you kind of sleep in the middle of the bed though to make sure you don't fall out."

Jackson sleeping on the couch would help to make Kat more comfortable. They would not have to sleep so close, and she would not wake up in his arms any more. On the other hand, Kat was not fond of the possibility of falling out of the bed. She had become dependent on Jackson to keep her from falling out. She was dependent on his protection.

Jackson sleeping on the couch lasted for almost a month. Kat's nightmares continued to reoccur several times a week. She woke up everyday thankful that she had not fallen out of bed. Part of her wished that Jackson was there to catch her in case she did fall, and to be perfectly honest, with herself even, part of her missed Jackson.

The couch was not a comfortable place to sleep whatsoever, but it made everything else easier. He didn't think about Kat physically as much with that extra distance between them. Maybe it wasn't that he didn't still think about her in that way, but out of reach was safer for her. It also made it easier to fight his own physical feelings.

# Chapter 8

One afternoon Jackson came home early from work. Kat was in the kitchen. Jackson walked into the kitchen just in time to catch Kat kick the stove.

"I don't think the stove will fight back. What did it do to deserve such violence?" Jackson asked.

"It quit. It just quit," Kat answered. "It won't heat up."

"Last week you said it was burning everything," Jackson reminded her.

"Last week it was. Last week you said you would fix it," Kat reminded him.

"Yes, I did, and I will," Jackson said.

"When?" Kat asked.

"As soon as I get a chance," Jackson answered.

"Oh great! So it may never happen!" Kat said angrily.

"It will happen. Give me time unless you want to fix it yourself," Jackson retorted.

"I don't have much of a choice, do I?" Kat smarted back.

"I got fired today," Jackson said very matter-of-factly.

"You got what?" Kat reacted.

"Take a chill pill. You know I jump from job to job constantly," Jackson said.

"So, do you have another job lined up?" Kat asked.

"Yes, I'm going to work with the local paramedics," Jackson answered.

"You, a paramedic?" Kat asked skeptically.

"Yeah, what's so hard to believe about that?" Jackson asked.

"You'll be saving people's lives?" Kat questioned.

"Yes, if I get the chance," Jackson said.

"OK," Kat said in a disbelieving tone.

"What's that supposed to mean?" Jackson asked.

"It's just a little far fetched to think of you saving people's lives," Kat answered.

"I've done paramedic work before; thank you very much," Jackson defended.

"Well, forget it. The stove is kaput," Kat complained.

"Sandwiches it is then," Jackson said lightly.

Jackson got out the bread while Kat got out the mayo and luncheon meat.

"What were you dreaming about last night?" Kat asked after calming herself down.

"Me? I wasn't the one screaming at the top of my lungs. When are you going to do something about those nightmares?" Jackson asked.

"Something? Like seeing a shrink?" Kat responded.

"Well, yeah. You could try seeing a mechanic, but I think you might get better results from a psychologist," Jackson smarted off.

"Absolutely not. I'm not crazy," Kat responded.

"Well, that is debatable, but this has nothing to do with your sanity. These nightmares are having a serious impact on your sleeping pattern. If the nightmare wakes you up, you don't go back to sleep. You're cranky all the time now. How is that affecting your attitude at school?" Jackson asked.

"It's not affecting my attitude at school at all. I don't take my problems out on the kids if that's what you're asking me," Kat replied.

"Fine, but you are tired. How long can you function like that?" Jackson asked.

"I don't know, Jackson. You tell me. How long can you function with that sore back?" Kat replied.

"My back's not sore," Jackson protested.

"It is so; it's sore from sleeping on the couch every night. I see you rubbing your back or trying to stretch it out anytime you think no one's looking," Kat accused.

"OK, I do. I have a sore back. Happy? What does that have to do with you going to see a psychologist? I need a chiropractic not a psychologist?" Jackson said.

"You need to quit sleeping on the couch," Kat smarted off.

"Maybe if you weren't having those stupid nightmares all the time, I wouldn't have to sleep on the couch," Jackson retorted.

"Right, it's not entirely my fault. Next I guess you'll tell me it's my fault you were talking in your sleep," Kat said.

"What are you talking about? I don't talk in my sleep," Jackson denied.

"Oh yes, you do. On nights that I'm woken up by a nightmare, I can hear you. You talk in your sleep quite often. Let's get one thing straight while we are at it. I am not responsible for your back problems. I did not tell you that you had to sleep on the couch. You did that to yourself," Kat pointed out.

"We couldn't keep sleeping in the same bed like that. I never knew when I would wake up with my hand all over you. I was uncomfortable and you were aggravated," Jackson reminded her. Jackson was more uncomfortable than Kat knew. He was not completely unaware of how beautiful she was, no matter what he tried to tell himself. Sleeping next to her night after night made it hard enough but to wake up with her in hand was too much. His back may be sore sleeping on the couch, but sleeping in the bed with Kat in his arms made him sore slightly lower down.

"So what! It's obvious that you weren't doing it on purpose, and you were only trying to help. I'll deal. There is no reason that you should be that uncomfortable that you would rather hurt yourself. Besides, I fell off the bed last night. That's what woke me up. I hit my head on the night stand. For a minute or two I thought I was going to have to wake you up and ask you to take me to ER for a CAT scan."

A grin spread across Jackson's face. "I'm serious," Kat continued. "I have a big knot. See; feel." Jackson felt the right side of Kat's head. Sure enough, she had a knot roughly the size of a golf ball. "It wasn't much fun. I would much rather wake up with your hands all over me than to wake up when my head slams against the nightstand," Kat said.

Jackson fought back his laughter. "So what you're saying is you think it would be better for both of us if I came back to bed?" Jackson questioned.

"Exactly, you do talk in your sleep though," Kat insisted.

"I do not," Jackson argued.

"We'll see," Kat said.

That night Jackson slept in the bed. If he was going to be sore and miserable in one way or the other, it was easier not to fight with Kat. She was the most stubborn person Jackson knew, and she could be unruly and difficult at times. Plus, Jackson did not want to take a chance on her falling out of the bed and hitting her head again. That knot was large enough that it worried him.

Kat did not have a nightmare, but Jackson did start talking. He was talking almost half the night. Kat finally threw a pillow over his head trying to drown out his voice.

"One night back in bed, and you're trying to kill me," Jackson commented the next morning.

"I was trying to shut you up so I could sleep. You were talking in your sleep," Kat told him.

"Yeah, right," Jackson reacted in denial.

"What have I got to do to prove it? What if I set out a tape recorder? Will you believe me if I get it on tape?" Kat asked.

"Sure, whatever," Jackson agreed.

That night Kat sat out a tape recorder, but the next morning there was nothing on the tape.

"I told you so," Jackson boasted.

"No, uh-uh, that was only one night. Now we rewind the tape and set it out again," Kat instructed.

"Fine," Jackson agreed.

Kat sat the tape recorder out again that night, but instead of catching Jackson, she had a nightmare.

"Is that me?" she asked.

"Absolutely," Jackson answered.

"Do I always sound that hysterical?" Kat asked.

"Every time."

"Wow, I'm squealing. Aren't I? What am I saying?" Kat asked.

"It's always the same. It's like you're fighting with someone. They are taking you somewhere against your will I presume, and you are arguing with them. You say things like: It's not fair. They don't understand. You can't leave right now," Jackson recalled.

"Leave where?" Kat asked.

"Don't know," Jackson answered.

"Have I been kidnapped?" Kat asked.

"Don't know. It doesn't really sound like it. It sounds like you know the person you're arguing with," Jackson answered.

"Really? You think?" Kat asked.

"Maybe, it is a dream; anything's possible," Jackson said.

"Yeah, you're right," Kat mumbled.

"Now do you see why I think you need to figure out what's going on?" Jackson asked.

"I'm not going to see a shrink," Kat proclaimed.

"It might help if you quit using the word shrink. You've got it in your head that only crazy people go to psychologists. That's not true. A lot of perfectly sane people see psychologists. It's how some sane people keep their sanity," Jackson said.

"What about you?" Kat asked.

"What about me? Have I ever seen a psychologist? Yes," Jackson said as if it should have been a given.

"Really?" Kat responded.

"Yeah, I've seen a lot of gruesome and disturbing things over the course of my career. Mental health has a way of becoming important. So, what do you say?" Jackson asked.

"I don't know. Let me think about it," Kat replied.

That night Kat started to rewind the tape and use the same tape. "Don't use that tape," Jackson stopped her. "Save that one with your nightmare on it. If you're going to continue this ridiculousness, get another tape."

Kat gave in without a fuss and got another tape. This time she caught Jackson but with a bit of a surprise. Both their voices were on the tape as follows:

"Melissa, Melissa, wake up."

"Jeb, shut up, and quit knocking on that window. Do you want to wake everyone up? I've been waiting out here forever. Where have you been?"

"I had to wake up Billy. He wouldn't get up. We have to hurry. Billy is going to meet us out by the front gate."

"Jeb, are you scared?"

"Yeah, are you?"

"Yes… Do you think this will work?"

"Yes, it has to."

"You know, we've never snuck off like this before."

"What else could we do? Hurry up. We have to beat sun up."

Jackson stared at Kat with a horrified look. "Melissa Kathleen… you took your aunt's last name, didn't you?"

"Yeah, but…" Kat responded.

"I'm so stupid. How did I miss it before?" Jackson mumbled. "I'm trained to catch everything, and I miss the most obvious stuff."

Kat stared back dazed and confused. "Don't you see?" Jackson asked. "No one has called me Jeb since I was ten. How could you have possibly known to call me that? Have you always gone by Kat?"

"I guess," Kat answered.

"What about before you came to live with your aunt?" Jackson asked.

"I don't know. I don't remember anything before I came to live with my aunt," Kat admitted.

Kat gathered her clothes and disappeared into the bathroom. When she came out, Jackson was still sitting on the side of the bed listening, studying the tape. Kat did not stop to talk. She did not even slow down. She did not know what Jackson was trying to get at with that tape, but he was very deep in some very serious thought. Kat could not remember ever seeing Jackson so upset. He looked sad; he looked hurt. Whatever he had been dreaming about had dredged up a lot of repressed emotions. Now he was trying to tie her in this somehow. Kat did not know what to do. She decided to do nothing until she had gotten more time to figure out the best way to handle this. She walked straight out of the bedroom without ever looking back.

When Kat got home from school that afternoon, Jackson was sitting at the kitchen table. He was not eating. He was not working. There was nothing on the table in front of him. He was not moving. He was not doing anything. His right forearm was lying on the table. His left elbow was propped up on the table with his head resting on his left hand. He was starring at the empty table. He did not even look up when Kat walked into the room.

"Hey, have you been here all day?" Kat asked.

Jackson looked up but seemed to look right through Kat. "Yeah, I took the day off," he answered.

"Is everything OK?" Kat asked.

"We need to talk," Jackson said.

"What's up?" Kat asked as she started taking clean dishes out of the dishwasher and putting them away.

"I know you said that you don't remember anything before you came to live with your aunt, but the thing is I've had that conversation before. Last night, whatever that was, I've had that conversation before word for word. I was seven. The girl I was with that night, Melissa, was seven. She was two months younger than me. You are two months younger than me. Her full name was Melissa Kathleen just like you. That night we were sneaking out to get married, or at least we thought we were getting married. It was our idea of marriage at the time anyway. Her parents worked for the CIA, and my parents worked for the CIA. We had both always been real observant of our surroundings. All the adults were constantly telling us that when we were together, they could not get anything by us. Her parents planned a visit to see her aunt. Her aunt was pregnant and having complications. Melissa and I both had a bad feeling that it was more than a visit. My older sister had gotten married the day before. We knew that my sister and her fiancé had to live with each other after they got married. The way Melissa and I figured it, we had to get married someday because we loved each other, and if we got married they couldn't separate us. So we paid very close attention at my sister's wedding so that we would know exactly what to do. Then we got Billy, the preacher's son, to help us. We thought since he was the preacher's son, it would work the same. We were shocked, to say the least, the next morning when her parents were not the least bit deterred. We put up a big fight argued till the very end. When they left, all I could do was stand there in the middle of the drive and watch. Her parents had to physically hold her down and buckle her into the back seat. I had never seen her throw such a fit. As soon as she was buckled in, she started jerking around and screaming at the top of her lungs the same way you jerk around and scream during your nightmares. When her parents came home, she was not with them. They said that she was going to live with her aunt from then on. They tried time and time again to explain that they felt it would be safer for Melissa if she stayed with her aunt, but I never forgave them. Kat, you said that you don't remember anything from before you came to live with your aunt, but that was pretty old not to remember anything at all. Melissa and I took martial art classes from the time we were about two and a half. Moves like the ones Owen described to me would have been easy for Melissa. You never missed a beat on that tape last night. How could you have recited that entire conversation that perfectly if you weren't there?"

"I don't know. Maybe I've heard you reciting it in your sleep so much that I just picked it up," Kat suggested.

Jackson put his head back on his hand and looked back to the empty table. "You don't remember anything? You don't remember where you lived? You don't remember your parents?"

"I already told you. I remember nothing. I got a couple birthday and Christmas cards from my parents over the first couple years. That is all I know about them. They've never been around. I vaguely remember them leaving my aunt's house. That was the last time I saw them. I can't even remember what they looked like. I see no reason to try to remember, and I don't like talking about it," Kat turned to walk out of the room.

"Just for the record, I don't like the name Jeb. That's why I started going by Jackson," he added.

Jackson did not mention any of those things again, but the friction grew between him and Kat. The tension was almost unbearable.

Kat would come in from school in the afternoons and start painting. Jackson would get home shortly after Kat and go to another room to work. First he fixed the stove. Then he patched the holes in the bedroom. Kat and Jackson would not eat together. The only time they would see each other is when they went to bed, and even then they would not speak.

One afternoon, when there was no other home improvement projects left outside the half bath or painting, Jackson came home and joined Kat in the living room to help paint.

At first they both worked in silence, but soon Kat broke the silence. "Jackson, have you ever killed anyone?"

"What do you think?" Jackson replied.

"I think it's possible," Kat said.

"Do you think I'm a murderer?"

"That's not what I said."

"What did you say?"

"I only said it was possible. I didn't say it was."

"Do you think I'm capable of cold blooded murder?"

"Why do you keep twisting my words?" Kat asked impatiently.

"Am I twisting your words?" Jackson asked.

"You most certainly are. That wasn't what I meant, and you know it," Kat snapped.

"Do I know that? What do you mean?" Jackson asked.

"You know full well what I mean! Have you ever killed anyone?" Kat shouted.

"Yes, I have," Jackson answered calmly. "Now that you know, what good does it do you to know?" Jackson asked.

"I don't know," Kat answered softly.

"What do you think?" Jackson asked.

"I don't know," Kat answered. The aggravation could be heard in her voice, and it was increasing fast.

"What does that make me?" Jackson asked.

"Shut up," Kat retaliated.

"Am I a cold blooded murderer now?" Jackson asked.

Kat threw the paint roller down and turned to face Jackson. "I never said that. You are the only one who said that. Why are you so hard to talk to? It's impossible to talk to you. I was serious. I just wanted to know. I never said anything about you. For all I know, it could have been self defense or some other reason that made it unavoidable. I never said you were a cold blooded murderer. I'm sorry I ever brought it up. The subject has been on my mind for a long while. All I wanted was to talk with you, but you make that into pure torture," Kat screamed.

"Is that all you've got?" Jackson asked.

"Why are you doing this?" Kat squealed hysterically.

"What am I doing?" Jackson asked.

Kat charged at Jackson but stopped herself. She turned to leave, but Jackson stopped her. "Where are you running to? Now would be the perfect time to show me some of those moves Owen spoke of."

Kat turned around swiftly and threw the first swing, but Jackson blocked her. She swung with the opposite arm, but Jackson blocked her.

"You'll have to do better than that to get the drop on me," Jackson boasted.

Kat kicked with her right foot. Her kick was chest high, smooth, and swift. It was a perfect kick. Jackson grabbed her leg. Kat spun around and with her left foot kicked Jackson in the head. Jackson let go of Kat's leg, and she fell to the floor.

Kat immediately jumped back to her feet. Jackson started to rub his jaw and said, "Not bad for someone who hasn't had a lesson in almost thirty years; impossible for someone who has never had a lesson in her life."

"Come on," Kat dared. "You have something you want to prove. Come prove it."

"I've already presented the evidence. You know the truth. I have nothing left to prove," Jackson replied.

"You started this. Don't back down now," Kat ordered him.

"I'm not backing down. I will not attack you, but I will block. If you want me, here I am. Come get me," Jackson challenged.

Kat shifted all her weight towards Jackson as she swung her right arm at his side, but he blocked her. Kat continued throwing one maneuver after another at Jackson. Jackson blocked about three out of every four moves Kat made.

Kat swept Jackson's feet out from under him causing him to fall flat on his back. Kat's only mistake was getting too close after knocking him to the ground. Jackson grabbed Kat's left ankle and pulled it out from under her. Kat came crashing down to the ground next to Jackson. Jackson rolled over on top of Kat pinning her down with her arms crossed over her chest. He leaned in close, face to face, close enough to kiss. Her hot breath brushed along his lips.

"Get off me," Kat growled. She straightened out her arms and jumped to her feet as she threw Jackson against the wall opposite her.

Kat stormed out of the room while Jackson climbed to his feet. Jackson followed Kat into the kitchen. She got a large pot and a skillet out of a cabinet and practically threw them onto the stove.

Jackson walked up right behind Kat. "Kat?" he said softly.

Kat turned around, and without a moment's hesitation she kissed him. It was all she could think about. It went well past want; she needed Jackson, needed his kiss, his touch. Jackson shoved her backwards hard against the stove and kissed back. They continued to kiss. Jackson slid his hands around her hips and lifted her up into his arms. Kat wrapped her legs around his waist, and he carried her to the bedroom without wasting an extra second. He had waited long enough for this, and he couldn't wait any longer.

Later… lying in bed, Kat asked, "Do you really think I'm that little girl from your past?"

"I have no doubt," Jackson answered.

"Jackson, I can't… I mean even if I was her at one time, I don't remember anything. I don't know how to be her," Kat said.

"Hey, hey, who's asking you to be?" Jackson said brushing the hair away from Kat's face. "That was a long time ago. A lot has happened since then in both our lives. Things change. Neither one of us can ever be who we once were. It's impossible. I know I can't go back after everything I've been through, and I don't expect you to."

Kat kissed Jackson and said, "I don't know who that little girl was, but that's not who I am."

# Chapter 9

A couple weeks later, Kat was just starting supper as Jackson walked in. She was making chicken and rice. For two weeks now, they had been a real married couple. Theirs, albeit, was a rocky relationship, but it was a relationship none the less.

Jackson walked up behind Kat. He said, "Hey," and kissed her neck.

"You're home early," Kat said with a smile.

"A little, I guess," Jackson agreed. "We were responding to a wreck today, and you'll never guess who the cop on scene was."

"Who?" Kat asked.

"Kelley White," Jackson answered.

"Oh, really," Kat replied.

"He said he just moved back a couple weeks ago, permanently this time. He asked about you," Jackson said.

Kat paused what she was doing. "What did you tell him?" she asked.

"I told him that you were doing fine as far as I could tell," Jackson answered.

"Is that all?" Kat questioned.

"No, I didn't mention anything about us getting married. I didn't think it was my place to tell your ex that you got married, especially since it's no secret that I never liked the guy," Jackson responded.

"Why don't you like him?" Kat asked.

"He's a chump who thinks he's really something. He's nothing but a big phony," Jackson answered. "It might be possible that I was the tiniest bit jealous too, but I definitely didn't know that at the time.

Kat smiled warmly and squirmed around in Jackson's tight embrace to face him. Then she rewarded him with a deep, passionate kiss.

The following Sunday Kelley was at church. He and Kat talked a long time just prior to the service.

"So how did he take it?" Jackson asked Kat on the way to lunch.

"How did who take what?" Kat responded.

"Yeah, right. You know what I meant. How did Kelley take it when you told him you were married?" Jackson asked again.

"It never came up," Kat answered casually.

"What do you mean it never came up? Hi, Kat, what's new? Oh, I got married. How does it not come up? Guess what. I got married. You just interject it. Oh by the way, I got married. It didn't come up. Maybe you just didn't bring it up," Jackson responded.

"No, I didn't bring it up. That is sort of a weird thing to bring up with an ex. You know? It's not like I went to great pains to hide the ring or anything. I didn't lie. It just didn't come up. I couldn't help it," Kat said defensively.

"So you plan to tell him?" Jackson asked.

"Of course. I just have to figure out how to tell him in case it never comes up," Kat answered.

"Are you going to wait for him to bring it up?" Jackson asked.

"I guess, until I figure out how to tell him," Kat answered.

"What's he going to do, walk up to you and ask 'Hey, Kat, did you get married while I was in Kentucky?'?" Jackson asked almost sarcastically.

"Now you're just being silly. Can't we talk about something different?" Kat responded.

"I wish we would. It didn't come up. That is the stupidest thing I ever heard," Jackson halfway mumbled.

"Then quit bringing it up," Kat instructed.

"Fine, I'm not saying a word, not another word," Jackson agreed, and that was exactly what he did. He did not say another word to Kat until halfway through lunch, and Kat had to pry that out of him.

"How's your food?" she asked.

"Fine." Jackson answered shortly.

"Just fine?" Kat pushed.

"Fine," he repeated.

For the next couple weeks Jackson would speak but was not particularly friendly. Not that things were ever abundantly friendly between Jackson and Kat. Jackson seemed to be more irritable than usual, more distant, and every week he would ask, "Did you tell him you're married?"

After three weeks of walking on egg shells, Kat finally asked, "How long are you going to keep up this childishness?"

"How long are you going to keep flirting?" Jackson responded.

"Flirting? What are you talking about?" Kat asked.

"I'm talking about you and Kelley White. Don't try to play innocent. You flirt with him all the time. You were flirting just this morning after church," Jackson replied.

"What?" Kat reacted.

"Don't deny it. Everyone saw you. That's the thing. You don't want to tell him that you're married. Whatever, I'm not saying a word, but you don't have to flaunt your flirting around the entire church. It makes me look like an idiot. What did I ever do to you? If you're going to continue flirting, at least do it in private," Jackson complained.

"I'm not flirting. How many times do we have to go over this? I want to tell him, but I don't know how to go about it," Kat argued.

"Oh bull! If you wanted to tell him, you would have already. When or even if you tell him you're married is not the issue. The issue is your open, unashamed flirting," Jackson snapped.

"I already told you I was not flirting! Be honest with yourself, Jackson. The issue here is not some hypothetical flirting. The issue here is your jealousy," Kat accused.

"What do I have to be jealous of, Kat? You don't even want to tell the guy you're married," Jackson shouted and stormed out of the house.

Kat followed after Jackson. "Where are you going?" she asked as he climbed into his truck.

"I don't know," Jackson yelled back. Jackson and Kat avoided each other as much as possible that week. Jackson got off a little early Friday. On his way home, he saw Kat pulled over by a cop, not just any cop, Kelley White.

Jackson was busily packing when Kat got home. "What are you doing?" she asked.

"What does it look like I'm doing? I've got the weekend off; I've got to get out," he answered.

"Can you do that?" Kat asked.

"It's only a weekend, Kat. I've got to get away. I saw you pulled over. Did he give you a ticket, or did the two of you have a nice little chat on the side of the road with his lights flashing?" Jackson almost growled.

"He asked me out, and I told him that we were married," Kat responded.

Jackson looked up at her and shook his head. He zipped up his bag and threw it on his shoulder.

"Where are you going?" Kat asked.

"Home," Jackson said.

"Where is that?" Kat asked.

"Home. Home is where my parents live. It's where I grew up. It's where you were born," Jackson answered.

"Can I go?" Kat asked.

"You want to?" Jackson responded.

"Yeah, I really do. I want to see this place that I don't remember," Kat answered.

"Get your stuff," Jackson said with a smile.

"Tell me about this place," Kat urged during the long drive.

"Well, uh, it's a base on the outskirts of town," Jackson said.

"What kind of base?" Kat asked.

"Everyone there is CIA and their families," Jackson started to answer.

"I didn't know that CIA lived on bases," Kat interrupted.

"They don't usually; this is an unusually hard core group of lifers. They're not hermits or anything. We went to school and attended church in town. I even had friends from school that would come spend the night with me when I was young. That's how Billy was able to meet us the morning you were leaving, but anyway, people who live there aren't excluded by any means.

They just prefer to live together with other CIA agents," Jackson explained.

"What about you?" Kat asked.

"No, I mean, don't get me wrong. I don't see anything wrong with the way they live, and I loved growing up there. I wouldn't have wanted it any other way. I had an advantage that most agents never had. I was taking martial arts at two. I was surrounded by CIA agents where learning was a natural and ongoing thing. I have a lifetime of experience that is irreplaceable, but now that I'm out on my own, I prefer to live among civilians. I don't really have a reason. It's just my personal preference," Jackson said.

The town was beautiful. It was elaborately and carefully landscaped. There was not any trash on the sides of the road anywhere to be seen. All the buildings were kept up and in perfect condition.

"That's the church where you were baptized," Jackson said pointing out the passenger side window.

Kat stared out the window at the church and said, "I was baptized at the church we go to now."

A little further down the road Jackson pointed out the driver's side window and said, "That ice cream shop right there is owned by one of the sweetest ladies I've ever met. Her kids run it now, but when we were young she still ran it. She loves kids, and at the time she didn't have any grandkids. Every time we would go in, she would always sneak us an extra scoop even though out parents told her not to. She knew our favorite flavor by heart. Mine was rocky road, and yours was…"

"Plain chocolate," they said simultaneously.

"You remember!" Jackson exclaimed.

Kat shook her head. "No, I know what my favorite ice cream is."

"That's the elementary school," Jackson said pointing to the right side of the road. "You only went there for kindergarten and first before they took you away… None of this looks the least bit familiar?" Jackson asked almost desperately.

Kat shook her head no silently.

"Stop the car!" Kat shouted as they drove through a large gate.

"What?" Jackson reacted as he slammed on the breaks.

Kat opened the door, threw off her seat belt, and hopped out of the truck. "I remember that tree," she yelled back to Jackson.

Kat ran down a slight hill to a huge oak tree next to a small creek. Jackson left his truck sitting in the middle of the road and ran behind Kat.

Kat spun around. "I remember this spot! I really do! I got my first kiss here."

A smile spread across Jackson's face immediately as he nodded his head. "It was the morning you left when we were trying to get married. It was a first real kiss for both of us, but it was nothing like this." Jackson pulled Kat into his arms and crushed his lips against hers.

"Jackson," Kat sighed. "I'm tired of playing games. I don't want you to feel jealous. I'm sorry if it appeared I was flirting with Kelley. I wasn't trying to flirt. I wouldn't disrespect you like that. When you said that was the way it looked, I should have respected you enough to back off, and I'm sorry."

"I shouldn't have flipped out like I did. You said you weren't flirting; I should have believed you. And, you were right; I was being childish."

"Jackson," Kat started, but Jackson cut her off with another breath steeling kiss.

"I always loved this tree. Come here." Jackson walked around to the other side of the tree. He squatted down. "There it is," he said pointing. "Look."

Down low on the tree trunk "Jeb and Melissa forever" was carved deep into the wood.

"That was us?" Kat asked.

"Yeah, that… was us… We better go. My parents are going to freak when they find out I got married without telling them," Jackson said. He stood and started back to the truck.

Kat followed Jackson. "You left your truck running in the middle of the road," she said surprised.

"Yeah, it's not that big a deal around here. There's a very different atmosphere here. There's nothing really to be afraid of. Who would be stupid enough to try anything? There's not a lot of traffic either," Jackson said.

Jackson pulled into a drive in front of a cute yellow house. There was a Harley Davidson motorcycle sitting in the front yard with a for sale sign. The front lawn was absolutely perfect.

To the left of the house there was a large white house with three cars in the driveway. All three cars were black. One was a Toyota. One was a Ford, and one was a Lexus. The lawn in front of the white house was just as perfect as the lawn in front of the yellow house.

To the right there was a small brick house on the opposite corner. There were no cars in the drive. The lawn was recently cut but not nearly as breathtaking as the lawns around it. The house was completely dark. There did not appear to be anyone home.

Jackson turned off the truck and got out. Kat climbed out of the truck as Jackson strode straight over to the bike. A man in his late fifties came to the front door grinning.

Jackson took the for sale sign off the bike. "Very funny, Dad," he said.

"Who's joking?" the man standing in the doorway replied. "If I had gotten any offers that thing would have been long gone."

"Where's Mama?" Jackson asked.

"I'm right here. No one is going to sell your motorcycle. Come on in, Jeb," she answered as she pushed past Jackson's dad.

"Mom," Jackson said accusingly as he started toward the house.

"Oh, sorry; I forgot," she responded.

"I've gone by Jackson for almost twenty-eight years. You didn't forget," Jackson corrected.

"I like the name Jeb. If I didn't like it, I wouldn't have named you Jeb," she said.

"You didn't name me Jeb, Mother. You named me Jackson Jebediah. If you didn't like the name, you shouldn't have named me Jackson," he pointed out as he walked in the door followed closely by Kat and shut the door.

"You look so familiar," Jackson's mom said looking at Kat. "Give me a minute. I never forget a face…"

"Mom," Jackson interrupted, but she ignored him.

"As I live and breathe, Melissa Cook; I haven't seen you since you were seven years old," she said.

"Mom," Jackson said impatiently.

"Come here, and give me a hug," she said and pulled Kat into an embrace.

"Mama!" Jackson said very aggravated, but she still continued to ignore him.

"May, your son is trying to talk to you. I think you should listen," Jackson's dad interceded.

"What is it, Jackson?" his mom asked in an agitated tone.

"She goes by Kat for starters. Secondly, she doesn't remember you, so you can let her go now. She doesn't remember any of us or anything else before she moved in with her aunt," Jackson explained with a smart attitude.

"That is not the least bit funny, smart butt. It can't be true… Can it, Melissa?" she responded.

"Kat, Mother, Kat," Jackson reminded.

"I'm sorry, Mrs. Johnson," Kat said.

"Oh my… Jackson take her across the corner. Let her see the house," Mrs. Johnson said.

"I thought the Cook's were gone," Jackson responded.

"Take the key," Mrs. Johnson said with a condescending tone.

"Right now? I really need to tell you something," Jackson said.

"Go on. You can tell me when you get back," Mrs. Johnson said.

"Mama, we just got here. I really want to talk with you about something kind of important," Jackson said.

"Don't argue with me, son," Mrs. Johnson snapped.

"Dad," Jackson called for help.

"May, your son is trying to tell you something, and I think you better sit down," Mr. Johnson said.

"Do you think I don't know when my own son has bad news?" Mrs. Johnson said.

"It's not necessarily bad news, but Dad's right. You might want to sit down," Jackson said.

Everyone followed Mrs. Johnson through the foyer to the living room where she sat down on the edge of a recliner. Mr. Johnson leaned up against the recliner. Jackson stood right in front of his mother. Kat moved to Jackson's right side. She took his hand in both her hands not sure if she was giving him encouragement or seeking her own.

"OK, there's no subtle way to say this, so I'm just going to say it. Kat and I got married. We sort of…"

"Gary, did you here that?" Mrs. Johnson interrupted. "It sounded like our son said that he got married without even telling his own parents."

"Uh… go to your room," Mr. Johnson said.

"Gary, he's thirty-seven years old. Sending him to his room doesn't really work anymore," Mrs. Johnson replied. She took a deep, slow breath. "Jackson, take Melissa home, and give us a minute to take this all in."

"Kat," Jackson corrected.

"I'm sorry. I honestly forgot. Go on, and show Kat around. Give me and your father a few minutes. Gary, breathe," Mrs. Johnson said in a very authoritative tone. This was her crisis mode. She was taking charge of the situation, trying not to lose control.

Kat squeezed her grip tightly around Jackson's hand. "Come on," he said.

Jackson grabbed a key off a hook hanging on the wall, walked out of the house, and started across the street. Kat was still holding Jackson's hand. Jackson pulled Kat's hands up to his face and kissed her hand. "Everything's OK. My parents like to think the major things though before they react. It's a pact they make with each other when I was born. They agreed never to let their strength and temper overpower them. I've been sent out to let them think countless times. They won't even look at me again until they are calm enough to talk it over," he said.

"How long will that take?" Kat asked.

"Don't really know. The longest they've ever taken was almost three hours. Well, this is it," Jackson said standing in front of the brick house.

"This is where I lived?" Kat asked nervously.

"Yep."

"Are you sure they're not here?"

"Nah, they're in Iraq right now. They're in the middle of a two year mission. They always have enjoyed the more complex assignments. There's not a soul here but us. Come on," Jackson replied. He unlocked the door and lead Kat inside.

Kat followed Jackson through the house, room by room. "None of this rings a bell, does it?" Jackson asked.

Kat shook her head no and followed Jackson down a small hall. "I haven't been back here since you left," Jackson mentioned. He opened a door at the end of the hall and walked in.

The walls were light pink. There was a white four post bed, a white dresser with a mirror, and a white chest of drawers. The bed had a pink patchwork quilt.

The carpet was white. In the middle of the room was a thick pink rug. Sitting on top of the rug was a blue bean bag chair that looked out of place. The window seal, the door, and the closet were painted white.

"This was your room," Jackson said.

"Wow, I must have been obsessed with pink," Kat commented.

"Not really. That was more your parents," Jackson said.

"What's the deal with the blue bean bag?" Kat asked.

Jackson laughed. "You were so stubborn. It was blue or nothing. Your parents wanted to get you purple, but they finally gave in. Your parents don't give in on much. In fact, they are the ones who taught me never to make deals. I'm not a negotiator. I work for the CIA. There is no deal, no compromise."

Kat walked around the room a couple minutes, silently looking around. Suddenly she walked straight to the corner of the room behind the door. She shut the door and got down on her knees facing the corner.

"Kat?" Jackson called.

Kat started pulling at the edge of the carpet.

"Kat, what are you doing?" Jackson asked.

"There's something down here," she responded.

Kat peeled up the corner of the carpet and picked up a piece of paper laying underneath.

"What is this?" she asked handing Jackson a folded piece of paper. There was a picture on the front obviously drawn by a child. It looked like a picture of a tree house.

Jackson took the paper and stared at it for a second. "I gave you this. What was it doing down there?"

"I don't know. I just knew it was down there," Kat admitted.

"It was a birthday card. I gave it to you for your sixth birthday. Look," Jackson instructed turning side by side with Kat so that she was able to see the card. "This is our tree house. We begged for a tree house forever. We told our parents that we would build it all by ourselves if they would get us the supplies. Since our birthdays are so close, that's what we got for our birthday. We built it during the two months between my birthday and yours."

Jackson opened the card up. On the left side there was a drawing of a person with the caption "Happy Birthday" up above. On the right side was another drawing of a person with "Love Jeb" written below. "That was supposed to be you," Jackson said pointing to the left side. Then he pointed to the right side. "That was supposed to be me."

Jackson turned the card over on the back where it said,

You are my favrit person in the hole world.
I am glad you are my frind.

"Nice spelling," Kat commented.

"Hey, come on. I was only six. Give me a break," Jackson reacted. "I made this thing all by myself with no help what so ever. I wanted it to be a surprise… I can't believe you kept this thing."

"I can't believe that I knew it was there," Kat said.

Jackson leaned over and kissed her. Then he pulled back and asked, "Do you want to see it?"

"See what?" Kat responded.

"The tree house," Jackson answered.

"Oh, sure, is it still around?" Kat asked.

"Of course, come on," Jackson replied.

Kat followed Jackson down the street and into the woods. They hiked though the woods for at least five minutes before Jackson stopped and held some tree branches back for Kat to duck under. She walked under the branches into a clearing. Jackson came through right behind her and said, "There it is."

The tree house was built between four trees. It was tall, at least six feet off the ground with only a rope hanging down used to climb in through a circular hole in the floor. There were four sides, a roof, and a door opening onto a small balcony surrounded by a rail. The whole structure still, thirty years later, looked strong and stable.

"Wow, we built that?" Kat asked.

"We sure did."

"At six years old."

"It was all us," Jackson bragged.

"I helped do that?" Kat asked unsure.

"Yeah, did half the work," Jackson said as he reached up and grabbed the floor of the tree house. He pulled himself up into the tree house. "You weren't always so prissy," he added.

"Who said I was prissy?" Kat retorted.

"I think that was me, just now," Jackson answered. He reached down with both hands to pull Kat into the tree house.

"Will that thing hold two adults?" Kat asked seriously.

"Yeah," Jackson answered as if it should have been a given.

"Two six year olds built a tree house strong enough to hold two adults?" Kat challenged.

"Yeah," Jackson answered again. "It could hold up more, but it would be a bit cramped. Are you coming up or not?"

Kat reached up and took Jackson's hands. He pulled her up into the tree house.

The walls were covered with drawings. In one corner several blankets were folded and stacked up neatly. In another corner was a medium sized box. In the third corner was a stack of empty plant pots.

"Who was the artist?" Kat asked.

Jackson rolled he eyes. "Some artist. That was me. You insisted on hanging them up. That box over there is full of paper, pencils, crayons, markers, tape, charcoal, and all kinds of stuff for drawing. You had been gone a couple years before I tried charcoal. The pots in the opposite corner were yours. You loved plants. You had plants lined up all across the balcony. I never had the green thumb you did. After all your plants died, I stacked them up. I was saving them for you. I was naive enough to believe that you would be back. I swore when you never came back, that I would never be that naive again. I guess I gave up too soon. It took thirty years, but you're back."

"Sort of. I had a green thumb?" Kat asked.

"Oh, yeah, you could make anything grow. Did you not ever plant things at your aunt's house?" Jackson asked.

"No, not unless it was a school assignment or something," Kat answered.

"That's a shame; you had a real gift. My art was a waste of time. I gave it up long ago when I realized that I would never be any good. What kind of things did you enjoy growing up?" Jackson asked.

"Well, I don't guess there was one certain thing. I played softball. I was in band," Kat said.

"Those are both group activities. What did you do when you were alone, something that was just for you?" Jackson asked.

"I don't know… What about you? You said that you gave up on art. So what is your thing?" Kat asked.

"I like hiking, climbing, camping, and that sort of thing, all the things I didn't get the chance to do growing up because my parents were so busy with work. I don't get much time for it, but I love it… I know what your thing is," Jackson said snapping his fingers.

"What is that?" Kat questioned.

"You do it all the time when you think you're alone or the only one on that end of the house. You sing constantly, and you're pretty good, by the way," Jackson said.

"I don't know how good it is, but I like to sing. So your thing can be anything that you do to relax when you're alone?" Kat asked.

Jackson nodded.

"Then hiking, climbing, and camping can't be your thing," Kat said.

Jackson forced a smile and said, "OK, explain."

"You shouldn't be hiking, climbing, or camping alone, so that can't be your thing. I know what your thing is," Kat told him.

"I'm listening," Jackson pushed.

"Anytime that you go for a run or workout, you always come back in a good mood," Kat said.

"It gets your adrenaline pumping. It's a natural stress relief, releasing endorphins," Jackson pointed out.

"Exactly, you do it alone, and it relaxes you. It's your thing," Kat told him.

"Alright, maybe. I do enjoy it," Jackson admitted.

Jackson and Kat sat in the tree house a long time talking.

"You ready to go?" Jackson asked.

"Sure, do you think it's been long enough?" Kat responded.

"Only one way to find out," Jackson answered and jumped down out of the tree house. He turned around to help Kat down, but she was already hopping down on her own.

Jackson and Kat took their time walking back to the house. Jackson opened the door very slowly and walked in very quietly as if he were trying to sneak in. "Mom? Dad?" he called softly.

"We're in here," Mrs. Johnson's voice came back.

Jackson shut the door, took Kat's hand, and walked into the kitchen with Kat. Mr. and Mrs. Johnson were sitting at the table when Jackson and Kat walked in.

"Jackson, we just don't know what to think," Mrs. Johnson said. "We called Meli… Kat's parents, and…"

"Mama!" Jackson shrieked. "You shouldn't have done that. You had no right to do that without asking Kat first."

"Oh, I'm sure Kat doesn't mind. Kat?" Mrs. Johnson said assuredly.

Kat tried to smile. "Actually, I would have preferred you didn't. I don't actually know them; I couldn't pick them out of a line up if I tried, and I'm still working through some issues about their cutting out like they did."

"Cutting out? Why wouldn't you know them? I don't understand," Mrs. Johnson stuttered.

"Kat, I hate to ask you to do this, but could you wait in the living room?" Jackson let go of Kat's hand and gave her a slight push.

Kat looked at Jackson strangely. "Sure, no problem." She went to the living room and took a seat on the couch, but she could still hear every word being said in the kitchen.

"Mama, I wish you had said something before you called the Cooks. Kat doesn't want to have anything to do with them. She pretty much hates them for abandoning her. Before you say anything, yes, I said abandon, and that's what I meant. She hasn't seen or heard from them in twenty-nine years, and the last time she did hear from them was a Christmas card when she was eight years old. The Cooks lied," Jackson said gradually getting louder.

"Did it ever occur to you that maybe Kat is the one lying?" Mr. Johnson said trying unsuccessfully to stay calm as he chimed in for the first time.

"I knew all this about Kat's relationship with her parents before we ever figured out who she was," Jackson replied.

"But you've known the Cooks all your life," Mr. Johnson insisted.

"So what? I knew Melissa a lot better than I knew them before they took her away, and now I know Kat better than I ever knew them. I'm telling you Kat is not lying," Jackson responded.

"Jackson, you're not thinking this through. Mark and Jane have been giving us up-dates over the years," Mrs. Johnson pointed out. "What about the dancing and the nursing?"

"It was all made up, Mama. Kat has never said a word about dance. She played softball, and she was in the band. Did the Cooks ever say anything about that? Kat's not a nurse; she's a teacher. Explain that. The Cooks always gave you the updates. Do you have any idea what they told me? Every time that they went to visit her, they would come back and tell me that she loved me but wasn't ready to come back. I have nothing left to hold on to except that Kat is telling the truth. If she really loved me, why wouldn't she at least send a phone number, an address, or something to stay in touch? Another thing, why didn't the Cooks ever tell us that she was going by Kat instead of Melissa?" Jackson argued.

"I don't know," Mr. Johnson maintained.

"What is not to know? You'll take their word over mine? If you don't believe me, get Kat in here. Question her yourself until you are satisfied. Kat?" Jackson called, but there was no answer. "Kat?" Jackson called a little louder but still no answer. "Kat?" Jackson screamed as he walked into the living room. "Kat!" Jackson screamed franticly.

Kat was no where to be found. Jackson pulled a cell phone out of his pocket and dialed Kat's number.

"Hello," Kat answered.

"Where are you?" Jackson asked in a panic.

"I'm across the street," Kat answered.

"Don't go anywhere. I'm on my way," Jackson responded.

Mr. and Mrs. Johnson followed Jackson to the door and watched as he sprinted across the street.

"What are you doing?" Jackson asked as he walked into the Cooks living room.

Kat was standing next to the mantel and holding a picture frame in her hand and crying.

"What's wrong?" Jackson asked.

"That's me," Kat said showing Jackson the picture.

"Yeah, I thought that we had already agreed that you and Melissa were definitely the same person," Jackson replied.

"Why would they tell you that I didn't want to come see you? Why would they do that?" Kat asked.

Without warning Kat hurled the picture at a wall. The glass shattered and flew everywhere. The frame itself broke into three pieces.

"What did I do?" Kat cried. She turned and pushed herself into Jackson's arms. "What did I do that was so bad? Why did they send me away? What was so wrong with me? Why did they decide after seven years that they did not want me anymore?"

"I don't know, Kat. I don't know. You were wonderful. You were so wonderful. I don't know why anyone wouldn't want you. I shouldn't have brought you here. Let's just go home," Jackson said softly.

Jackson started to guide Kat back outside, but his parents were standing in the open doorway.

"I'm so sorry," Mrs. Johnson said.

"We had no idea," Mr. Johnson added.

Jackson shook his head. "There was no way you could have known. I saw the fit Melissa threw the day she left, and still I never dreamed it was all a lie. It wasn't until after Kat and I were married that I figured out the truth," Jackson admitted softly.

"We would love to get to know Kat all over again if you would give us the chance," Mrs. Johnson said.

"Mama, we can't stay. It's just too hard,"
Jackson replied.

"May, let them go. Can't you see what Mark and Jane
have done to her? We will visit them. There is no sense
in her having to endure this," Mr. Johnson stepped in.

It was already late. They wouldn't get home until
tomorrow, but Jackson and Kat left anyway. Jackson
helped Kat into the truck. He hugged and kissed his
parents good-bye, and then Jackson and Kat left. Kat
cried herself to sleep. Jackson drove all night long.

# Chapter 10

The next few weeks were long and hard for both Jackson and Kat. Kat struggled to get through her day to day routines. Jackson did not know what to do to help her. She was trying too hard to keep going, but summer was close.

During the summer when Kat was home alone most of the day, Jackson would rush home. He spent as much time as he could at home with Kat. Kat did not want to leave the house much at all. Jackson had to practically make her continue to get out of the house for things that used to be a regular for them such as singles game night.

Even though Jackson and Kat were no longer singles, they were still very much involved with most that the singles did. Until lately, game night remained a constant for Jackson and Kat even though it was quickly becoming an uncomfortable situation.

Kelley White had rejoined game night. He started out the first couple times back playing Clue. The tension between Jackson and Kelley was volatile to say the least. Their competitiveness hit an intensity that made everyone at the table jumpy. Kat was wedged right between Jackson and Kelley. Every time Kelley would bump into Kat, Jackson would shoot him a threatening look. Kat had never seen Jackson so hostile. She barely moved for fear that she might bump into Kelley and set off Jackson.

Finally whether he was frustrated or scared, Kelley moved on to a different game. Things were just beginning to get back to normal when Kat gave up wanting to participate. Jackson and Kat's attendance became very sporadic depending on Kat's mood. Even when Kat's mood was fairly pleasant, they only went if Jackson coerced her into getting out of the house for a little while.

One night in particular, Jackson almost forced Kat out of the house for game night. She had not left the house at all in almost a week, and Jackson felt she had to get out of the house for her own sake. That night Kat was quiet, very distracted, very much in her own world. Anytime anyone spoke to her they would have to call her name at least three times. Each time Kat's turn rolled around, Jackson would have to nudge her with his elbow.

"Kat, are you OK?… Kat… Kat!" Jackson called. Kat looked over at Jackson without response. "Kat, are you OK?" he repeated.

"I'm fine," Kat answered.

"Kat, I just won three straight rounds with no challenge and you haven't marked off the first thing on your paper. Are you sure you're alright?" Jackson asked.

Kat nodded, but never said a word. "Do you want to call it a night? Let's just go home," Jackson suggested.

Kat nodded again and stood up to leave. Jackson stood up and apologized for the interruption.

"Is she going to be OK?" Mrs. Judy asked.

"Oh yeah, she's fine. She's a little distracted lately, but she's fine," Jackson lied.

Jackson opened the door and helped Kat into the truck (Kat had not driven anywhere once since school let out.); then he walked around and got into the truck.

"Kat, I think we need to talk," Jackson said.

"Talk," Kat responded.

"I'm really worried about you. Since we got back from the base, you hardly talk. Since school let out, you almost never leave the house. If you do leave the house, it's because I made you, and I don't know whether I'm doing the right thing or not. I hate to see you sit around the house day after day. When you leave the house, you are so out of it that I feel guilty for making you go out like that. Some days you don't even get out of bed. This thing has gotten to the point that I'm scared to leave you alone," Jackson confided.

"That's ridiculous," Kat said half-heartedly.

"Kat, I'm serious. You are really scaring me. Please, don't blow this off," Jackson pleaded.

"I'm not. There's nothing to blow off. You're over reacting. I'm just spending the summer being lazy. This is my time off. Lay off," Kat defended.

"I'm not over reacting. This isn't like you," Jackson insisted.

"Oh yeah, because you know me so well. You know me better than I know myself," Kat said with angry sarcasm.

"Sometimes," Jackson mumbled under his breath.

Neither of them said another word during the ride home. When they got to the house, Kat went straight to the bedroom and shut the door. Jackson sat down in a recliner and started watching TV. No one moved for almost forty-five minutes. When Kat did finally emerge from the bedroom, Jackson, trying to keep down the confrontation, did not even look at her. Kat walked right past Jackson. She picked up the remote and muted the television.

Kat sat down in Jackson's lap and said, "Tell me about myself." Her eyes were red and swollen. It was obvious that she had been crying.

"What?" Jackson responded caught off guard.

"Tell me about myself when I was little. What was I like?" Kat asked.

"You mean tell you about Melissa? Well, I can definitely see similarities. Melissa… you were determined, smart, observant, resourceful, loyal, loving. I know you can't see it right now, but maybe everything you went through wasn't all bad. For instance, you are a wonderful teacher; teaching would never have crossed Melissa's mind."

"You've never seen me in the classroom," Kat interrupted.

"No, I haven't, but I have seen the way the kids come running up to talk with you when they see you out in the community. It doesn't matter what you were doing when they ran up to you; you always stop to talk with them. I've heard the parents of your students brag about how much their kids learned in your class. I've seen how much time and care you put into your work here at home. You probably bring home more homework than your students. I hope so at least. You really shouldn't give the kids that much homework… Is that a smile? Oh I haven't seen one of those in so long." Jackson stopped to kiss Kat. "If you had stayed at the base, you would be working for the CIA right now. We would be partners, and you would have missed your calling. I'm as sure of that as I am anything. Plus your aunt did a colossal job mellowing you out. You were so bossy. You had good intentions, but you were way too controlling."

"Did I try to control everyone including my parents?" Kat asked.

"Oh, no. Uh-uh, you respected adults very much especially your parents. Is that what this is about?" Jackson asked.

"Kind of, is that why my parents didn't want me around?" Kat asked.

"Of course not. Kat, don't do this. You were exactly who they had created. Your mom pushed you to take care of everyone, and they both pushed you to be strong; it is no wonder that you were controlling and bossy. Your parents told me time after time that you were living with your aunt because it was safer, and I believe that. Your dad was always leery of raising children on the base. He had a genuine fear that raising you on the base around all the masculine, hard core CIA agents, you might grow masculine and wind up a lesbian. After you left, your parents used to brag to mine about how good a dancer you were which is a very girl thing to do. With your aunt you were safe from the danger of CIA work, you were safe from the gruesomeness of CIA work, and you were safe from the chance of turning gay. You were left with your aunt because of your parents' paranoia. You didn't do anything wrong," Jackson argued. "I don't think I ever really forgave them for that. What they did was cowardice. Parents don't do that; good parents don't anyway. It was never said that they had to live at the base or else. Fact of the matter is that a very small minority of agents live on bases. I only know of one other such place. They didn't have to stay there if they didn't think it was right for you. They had the option to leave, family intact, but they chose to send you away instead. That was their mistake that we all suffered for. You didn't do that. You didn't do anything wrong."

"Do you really believe that?" Kat questioned.

"With all my heart," Jackson answered.

"Then why didn't they ever come to visit, call, or anything?" Kat challenged.

"You didn't want to leave the base. You didn't want to stay with your aunt, and all I saw was the fit before they officially told you that it wasn't just a visit. Maybe it was just too hard to have to leave you over and over again," Jackson offered.

"Jackson," Kat said in a correcting tone. He was trying to placate her, and she knew it.

"I don't know, Kat. I don't know. If I had known where to find you, I would have visited you all the time," Jackson said and kissed her.

"That's completely different, and you know it," Kat accused. "You thought Melissa could do no wrong. Look at how you fell all over yourself getting to me when you figured out I was her."

"Is that really what you think?" Jackson asked. "I'm glad that we are finally talking about this. You have a lot of misconceptions. Believe me; I did not think that Melissa could do no wrong. I can give you a long list of faults. Secondly and most importantly, I love you, Kat. I love who you are now. I was falling for you before I ever put two and two together. Even if you weren't Melissa, I would still love you."

"Do you think I might not be Melissa?" Kat asked.

"Oh, Kat, get real! I never told you where we had our first kiss, and I had no idea about the card underneath the corner of the carpet," Jackson reminded her.

"Yeah, you're right," Kat admitted. "What is your list of faults with Melissa?"

"She was bossy for starters. Oh my goodness, were you bossy. You had good intentions, but crud; let me make my own mistakes every once in a while. You wanted to take care of everyone and like I said, you were just too controlling. Your friends from school were so annoying. I couldn't stand them. Anytime that they would come over to play, I would hide out in the tree house. We had a pact to never take anyone else to the tree house, so I always had somewhere to go hide away. The ironic part is that I dated half of them later in life," Jackson admitted.

"What was wrong with my friends?" Kat asked.

"Nothing. They were just real girly. They only wanted to play things like dolls or dress up. You actually owned a ton of Barbie dolls. Your dad used to buy them all the time, but you kept them hidden under your bed unless your friends came over to play. I guess I had not learned to stand girls yet. You were my only female friend back then. I always hid from your friends, but you would come out to play with mine. My friends were all boys, and they liked playing things like sports, wrestling, cars. Oh, wrestling, that's another one. You would beat all my friends up. I would ask you to take it easy on them, but you would tell me that it was not your fault if they were all big babies," Jackson recalled with a grin.

"So I was a rough and tumble tom boy," Kat commented.

"Sometimes, but you could be real girly at times too. You thought you always had to dress cute. You just had to. Even if we were just going outside to play on Saturday afternoon just the two of us, you would not leave the house until you made sure you looked cute. You still do. You had a nice blend of girly and tom boy. You really were a well rounded person," Jackson said.

"Were?" Kat questioned.

"Yeah, you were a well rounded person. Now you are a prissy girl," Jackson replied.

"That is the second time that you've called me prissy. What is so prissy about me?" Kat asked.

"Everything about you is prissy," Jackson stated.

"Like what?" Kat challenged.

"What about this?" Jackson asked tugging at Kat's shirt. "What is this?"

"My pajamas," Kat answered.

"Your pajamas, you're ready for bed then, huh?" Jackson pushed.

"Yes."

"You're ready for bed? Your hair is neatly combed. There's not a hair out of place. You are neat and fresh. There is not a spec of dirt anywhere on you, and you smell just as good as you did when you stepped out of the shower this morning." Kat rolled her eyes, but Jackson ignored her and just kept talking. "It is OK to relax from time to time. You don't have to look perfect all the time. Look at your pajamas. What is up with your pajamas? They are pink with pink flowers and pink lace. Pink, pink, pink! Do you see in pink and lace? Is that lace honestly comfortable to sleep in or is it just cute?"

"OK, OK, you've made your point," Kat said as she climbed out of Jackson's lap.

Kat started out of the room, but Jackson called out, "You even walk prissy."

Kat spun around. "What's wrong with the way I walk?"

"You're twisting my words again. Why do you always to that?" Jackson mocked in a prissy voice. "I like the way you walk," he added.

Kat smiled slyly then she turned slowly and walked out of the room giving it as much emphasis and drawing as much attention as possible. Jackson hopped out of the recliner and chased after Kat.

Kat woke up the next morning in what seemed to be a much better mood. After that night, Kat always seemed to be in an excellent mood at home, but as soon as they left the house, she was automatically back in her rut.

# Chapter 11

"Kat, you haven't said anything about that teacher's conference down in Destin. Aren't you planning to go this year?" Jackson asked.

"I don't think so," Kat answered.

"Why not?"

"It's the same thing every year. I just don't feel like going all the way down there and sitting through all that this year," Kat answered.

"Oh, OK, what do you think about going down there on vacation with me. It would be just the two of us and a good excuse to get out of here for a little while," Jackson suggested.

"Just the two of us?" Kat questioned.

"Yeah, just the two of us. Think about it, a nice, quiet weekend to ourselves with no interruptions."

"No interruptions?" Kat challenged.

Jackson was sitting in the recliner. He had been working all morning and had papers stacked up all around him. Kat was lying across the couch. She had been cleaning all morning and had only recently quit.

Jackson looked across at Kat with a curious look. "No interruptions, just you, me, and the beach," he lied smoothly but not trying to hide the truth on his face.

"Oh, so we aren't following anyone down there, like John Doe?" Kat asked knowingly.

Jackson picked up a piece of paper, wadded it up, and threw it at Kat. "Shut up! At least I'm trying!"

"Oh yeah, you're trying, and you're so romantic," Kat laughed.

Jackson tried hard not to smile, and he avoided looking at Kat.

"Toss me the controller," Jackson said.

"I'm watching this," Kat argued.

"No you're not; toss me the controller," Jackson repeated.

"If you want it, come get it," Kat pushed.

"Oh, no, I wouldn't dream of it. If you want to see this infomercial, far be it for me to interrupt. Please, watch on," Jackson teased.

A few minutes later Jackson stood up and started toward the controller.

"Hey! I'm watching that," Kat exclaimed.

"Shut up," Jackson reacted.

"You like that phrase today, don't you?" Kat pointed out. "You know, in my classroom, we don't say that."

"We're not in your classroom," Jackson retaliated.

Kat kicked Jackson in the butt as he walked past on his way back to the recliner. He turned to look at her. She looked up at him defiantly.

Jackson set the controller down calmly and sat on Kat's legs careful to keep his full weight off her so not to crush her.

"No, Jackson! Prissy girls don't fight, especially with boys," Kat protested.

"Too late," Jackson said as he grabbed both Kat's flailing wrists. He pinned her arms down. "You should have thought about that before you started it."

"Get up!… Let me up!… What are you doing?" Kat screamed.

"I'm going to Florida. I was just wondering if you were going to come along," Jackson said.

"Yeah, I'll go with you if it means that much to you. When are we leaving?" Kat asked.

"Saturday."

"Saturday? Jackson, isn't today Thursday?" Kat reacted.

"Yeah so?"

"Short notice, isn't it?" Kat pointed out.

"You'll get used to it after a while," Jackson assured her. Then he leaned down to kiss her. As he deepened the kiss, all thoughts of the TV or the remote disappeared.

Kat spent all day Friday packing and getting the house cleaned up so that they could leave. She had such short notice that she was cleaning like a person possessed trying to get everything done in time.

"Why are you cleaning so hard?" Jackson asked. "We won't even be here for almost a week."

"I can't stand the idea of leaving the house a mess," Kat admitted.

"Compulsive," Jackson mumbled under his breath.

"I heard that!" Kat shot. "It's not compulsive; it's orderly. Besides wouldn't you rather come home to a clean house?"

"I would rather come home to a straightened up house, sure, but I really couldn't care less if the floors have been vacuumed, swept, and mopped. In fact I probably won't even notice stuff like the floors or the windows or the curtains, or any other of the other compulsive cleaning that you are doing when we get back home. I don't know why you are wasting your time dusting; all that dust will be back by the time we get back," Jackson pointed out.

"If I don't dust now, it will be twice as thick when we get back," Kat argued.

"Oh big loss," Jackson teased, and he walked out leaving Kat to her cleaning.

By Saturday Kat was so exhausted she slept half the way there. When she woke up, she had a big question on her mind. "Jackson, I know it's a little late to be asking now, but how exactly can we afford this trip?"

"Don't worry about it," Jackson replied very casually.

"We can't can we?" Kat said.

"We'll work it out," was Jackson's only answer.

"How?" Kat challenged.

"I don't know yet, but we'll figure something out. We'll do what we have to. This trip was kind of important, Kat," Jackson answered.

"I know it was important, but where is the money going to come from?" Kat responded. "Vacations use a chunk of money. We don't have an extra chunk of money just lying around."

"No joke. I said we would figure something out, and I will. Don't worry about it. I will handle everything when we get back. Put it out of your head, and try to have fun," Jackson said.

"You don't know me very well, do you?" Kat replied.

"Just try," Jackson pleaded. He knew better. He did know Kat that well, and he knew that she would worry about the money until she was sick with it.

"Oh, I'll try, but I'm not making any guarantees. I'm not going to get that off my mind," Kat admitted.

Jackson reached across the console for Kat's hand and asked, "Have fun anyway?"

Kat took Jackson's hand and answered, "Sure."

The hotel was gorgeous inside and out. The rooms were spacious. The bathroom was huge with a walk-in shower and a whirlpool tub.

"Jackson," Kat said in a demanding voice.

"What?" Jackson asked.

"We can't afford this. What did you do, find the most expensive hotel you could?" Kat demanded.

"Yeah, that's it exactly. How did you know?" Jackson taunted.

"Jackson, I'm serious," Kat whined.

"So am I; everything will be just fine if you will relax. This isn't the first time I've had to spend money that I didn't have. Somehow it always works out; have a little faith, Kat. We'll work everything out when we get back, and it will be fine. You'll see," Jackson insisted.

He wrapped his arms around Kat's waist and pulled her close. "Kat, trust me."

"You realize that if things get much tighter, we'll have to give up eating," Kat insisted.

"Yeah right, speaking of eating, I'm starving," Jackson said. Kat was tense inside Jackson's arms. He knew without a doubt that she was not going to relax as long as she was still worried about the money. "I do have more money that we can tap into if we have to, but for appearances sake we need to avoid that as much as possible," he reluctantly admitted.

"What money?" Kat asked.

"Oh come on, Kat. Did you seriously think I was that broke on a CIA salary? In reality I make good money; I easily triple your salary. It's easier to pretend that money doesn't exist, because it can't exist for us right now. Quit worrying about money. Let me handle it, and everything will be fine," Jackson explained.

"OK," Kat agreed easily, but she looked suspicious.

"Perfect. Let's go find something to eat now," Jackson suggested.

"We've been riding all day," Kat pointed out.

"So, what does that mean? We quit eating?" Jackson reacted.

"Can I get cleaned up first?" Kat asked with an obvious attitude.

"Whatever," Jackson replied.

Kat was stepping out of the shower when she heard a knock at the door. Jackson opened the door. "Hank, what are you doing here?"

"I saw you down in the lobby. Where's your wife?"

"She's in the shower," Jackson answered. "Can I do something for you?"

"Yes, actually, meet me for dinner across the street in half an hour, my treat."

"If you're paying, how could we refuse?" Jackson replied.

"I'll see you there," the man said and left.

Kat opened the bathroom door. "Jackson?"

"Don't look so worried. I just saved us money," Jackson responded.

"I don't think I want to eat with John Doe, and I wasn't supposed to know his name," Kat reminded him.

"I didn't tell you his name. Did I? Is it my fault that you were eavesdropping?" Jackson asked.

"You were standing on the other side of the door. How could I keep from hearing you?" Kat pointed out.

"Yeah, yeah, finish getting dressed," Jackson said and kissed Kat. He meant to give her a swift kiss and move her along to get ready, but it turned into a lingering kiss that seemed to go on forever.

Jackson and Kat spotted John Doe right away as they walked into the restaurant. John Doe stood up to greet them. "Hi, Kat, isn't it? I don't think that we have been properly introduced. I'm Hank Heart, and this Roxy," he said gesturing to a busty young blonde with him. The girl gave a very nervous grin. "Please, have a seat," Hank added. "So tell me, Jackson; what brings you down to Florida?"

"Vacation, Hank. Living the good life. Just enjoying my wife's company," Jackson answered. "You know how it is, man."

"Do you mind if I ask you what brings you down here?" Kat asked.

"I'm vacationing too, away from my wife," Hank said with a wink.

Kat nodded slightly as Jackson chuckled.

"He's joking, Kat. Hank's not married," Jackson clarified.

"Oh," Kat uttered sheepishly. "Mr. Heart…"

"Please, call me Hank. I feel like I know you so well already. I heard so much about you from Jackson before he left."

"About that, why did you want to eat with us and offer to pay even?" Kat asked.

"I like Jackson. He's a hard worker, very efficient. I owe him more than I paid him," Hank answered.

"Well, I'm glad to hear he worked a little faster for you than he does at home," Kat commented giving Jackson an accusing glance.

"Stop with the flattery, Hank. Kat thinks I'm a lazy bum, and I like it that way," Jackson laughed.

"Sorry, Kat, but there is nothing lazy about your husband," Hank said. "It broke my heart when Jackson told me he was quitting. It meant…"

"Quitting?" Kat interrupted. She turned her full attention to Jackson. "Wait. What? He just said you quit?"

"I heard him," Jackson responded.

"Why would he say that?" Kat asked.

"I don't know, Kat. Why do you think he would say something like that?" Jackson replied. "Do you think that might could be what happened?"

"Why?" Kat asked sternly.

"I don't know. I just got tired," Jackson answered.

"I'm not asking why you quit," Kat explained.

"Can we talk about this later?" Jackson urged.

"I didn't mean to cause any trouble," Hank said.

"No, you're fine; Kat's just over reacting," Jackson said.

"I'm not over reacting, but none of this is your fault," Kat reassured Hank.

"Of course not, let's just drop it," Jackson suggested.

The rest of the meal was an uncomfortable one. Roxy barely said two words, and when she did speak, she only proved that she was very much an airhead. Kat did not have very much to say either. Jackson and Hank kept conversation going. They laughed a lot, mainly at inside jokes that Kat and Roxy knew nothing about. The meal was pretty much a bore for Kat and Roxy. Lucky for them the food was good.

Everything seemed to drag. As the meal wrapped up, conversation did not. Jackson would not let it. He was literally avoiding the conversation's end. He was not ready to go back to the hotel and face Kat's wrath. It started getting late fast. Finally Hank terminated the conversation in order to get back to his room and get some rest.

Jackson and Kat started a slow quiet walk back to their own room. At one point, Jackson reached out for Kat's hand, but Kat retracted her hand before Jackson could reach her. Jackson did not say a word nor did he try anything else until they got back to the room.

"Kat," Jackson said softly when they got back, but Kat turned into the bathroom slamming the door in his face.

Kat came out of the bathroom and still did not say a word. She never looked at Jackson. She picked up her bag and started unpacking. Jackson watched her silently, but she never looked up. Kat changed into her pajamas and climbed into bed.

"Kat?" Jackson said, but Kat did not respond. She did not acknowledge him at all. "So now what?" Jackson asked. "You're going to give me the silent treatment?" Jackson waited a minute, but Kat still would not respond. "That's real mature, Kat. Come on. Let's be reasonable."

Kat jerked up and turned toward Jackson. "Reasonable? What's reasonable, Jackson? I don't know what to say. How mature was it when you lied?"

"How would you have reacted if I had come home and said 'Hey, Kat, I quit my job today'?" Jackson questioned.

"I don't know. You never gave me the chance," Kat pointed out.

"I know you, Kat even if you don't believe me. You are a worrier. Be honest with yourself. You would have freaked out," Jackson said.

"Maybe so, but you should have told me," Kat insisted.

"Why? We got through it OK, and you never had to deal with the panic. You trusted me to find another job. Could you have trusted me like you did if you had known that I quit?" Jackson asked.

"Of course," Kat responded.

"Kat," Jackson said in a very challenging tone.

"OK, fine, I don't know. You never gave me the opportunity, but I know I can't trust you now," Kat replied.

"What? That's ridiculous. It's ludicrous… You know what? That's fine. If you want to be childish, then be that way. No skin off my back," Jackson snapped. He lay down in bed facing the opposite direction from Kat and started mumbling under his breath. "I did that for your sake, ungrateful… If I was going to lie for my own benefit, I wouldn't say I got fired… The silent treatment? How old are you?"

Both Jackson and Kat fell to sleep without another word, but only two hours later they jerked awake. Kat had one of her usual nightmares at a violent pace. As was his routine, Jackson rolled over and threw his arm over Kat. She was flailing around uncontrollably with both fists swinging. She punched Jackson right in the face.

"Owe! Wake up! Kat, get up! You just slugged me," Jackson started patting his left eye. "Oh, Kat, that's going to turn into a black eye. How am I supposed to explain that one? It wasn't just any girl who gave me a black eye. It was my wife!"

"I'm sorry," Kat apologized.

"Talk about timing. We go to bed fighting, and I wake up with a shiner," Jackson commented.

"I've got to get out of here," Kat said.

"I was only teasing. I don't seriously think you did it on purpose," Jackson defended.

"I know. I just need some air," Kat explained as she pulled some clothes over her pajamas.

"I'll go with you," Jackson offered.

"No! No, no, that's OK. I'm just going to walk down the beach a little way and come back. I'll be fine. I need to get away for a few minutes, away from everything, including you," Kat responded.

Jackson sat stunned. He did not say a word. He did not try to stop her. He sat and watched her walk out the door.

The hotel was asleep. There was no life anywhere. No one was stirring. Kat silently made her way down the hall, through the hotel, and out to the beach. She strolled slowly along the shore. Before she noticed, Kat had gone a long way.

Kat had walked nearly two miles when she noticed someone running behind her. Kat stopped and watched the runner until he came into view. "Jackson, what are you doing?" she called.

"Coming after you," Jackson answered.

"Jackson," Kat whined. "I told you I needed to get some air a minute or two."

"I gave you a minute. I really did. Yeah, I sat there a minute before I realized that this wasn't about the nightmare. Is it?" Jackson asked.

"Not entirely," Kat admitted.

"I knew it. This is about earlier. Isn't it?" Jackson asked. "You're blowing this out of proportion. Yeah, I lied, but I had good cause. I did it for the greater good. That's the way I have always done things."

"That's the problem. You can't do things that way anymore, at least not with me. I will try my best to be understanding and open minded, but you have got to be honest with me. If you think about what you did, you weren't open minded yourself. It was very close minded when you assumed that I wouldn't understand," Kat put forth.

"Fine, that's…"

"Shhh," Kat interrupted and grabbed his arm.

Jackson looked around, and a man stepped out of the shadows.

"How do I keep running into you?" Hank asked.

"I don't know. Are you following us?" Jackson asked only half jokingly.

"I was just wondering the same thing about you, Jackson," Hank replied.

"You scared me to death," Kat added.

"I sure didn't mean to scare anyone. I couldn't sleep, so I was taking a walk. I ran into you and couldn't help but overhear that you were arguing again. I hope it's not on my account," Hank said.

"Don't flatter yourself, Hank," Jackson laughed. "It has nothing to do with you. In fact, it's not even really an argument. It's more like a long overdue conversation. Isn't that right, Kat?"

"I suppose so," Kat agreed.

"Well, I don't mean to keep you," Hank said. He turned and continued on his way as his phone rang. "Give me your spiel," he answered.

Jackson and Kat turned around and headed back toward the hotel hand in hand.

"That's a rather unusual way to answer the phone, don't you think? I've heard someone answer the phone that way before, but I can't remember who right now," Kat whispered.

"Well, that doesn't do much good, does it?" Jackson responded.

"Don't start," Kat warned.

"I'm not starting anything," Jackson insisted.

"Then lose the attitude," Kat instructed.

"I don't have an attitude. I'm tired," Jackson said. "Let's just go back to the room and get some rest."

That was the last time during the trip that Jackson or Kat spoke with Hank Heart, but everywhere they went there he was. Jackson kept a close eye on Hank but never approached him. They stayed out of Hank's sight for the most part.

# Chapter 12


Jackson and Kat returned home, and the remainder of the summer faded away quickly. Before long Kat was returning to school for pre-service.

Pre-service was the same thing year after year. They sat through the same meetings every year with the same speakers and the same old, tired speeches. Pre-service days were merely meetings that must be endured in order to get each school year started. Kat hated sitting through all the boring, stale meetings, but this year was different. This year Mrs. Judy was scheduled to speak the last day. Mrs. Judy's high spirited, fun loving disposition would be a welcome change of pace. Kat could not wait. Mrs. Judy's presentation ought to be useful information.

Kat was talking with Mrs. Judy prior to the start of her presentation. "How is everything at the Johnson home?" Mrs. Judy asked.

"We're doing good. How about you?" Kat returned.

"Doing good; doing good," Mrs. Judy answered. "How's the house coming along?"

"We've actually got everything done now except for the half-bath. We've got the bath shut off, and Jackson is avoiding it. He looks for any excuse he can find to put it off, but the rest of the house looks great. I'm real pleased with the house," Kat explained.

"Well, I'm glad to hear that. I actually want to talk to you about something a little later. Don't let me forget," Mrs. Judy said.

Kat started to nod her head, but was interrupted by Mrs. Judy's cell phone.

Mrs. Judy pulled the phone out of her pocket and glanced down. "Oh, excuse me a minute, Kat," she said and turned to walk away, but Kat could hear her answer the phone as she walked away. "Give me your spiel."

Kat spun around quickly and turned a corner. She pulled out her own phone and tried to call Jackson. Jackson did not answer. Kat hung up and tried again, but Jackson still did not answer. This time Kat left a message. "Jackson, call me back ASAP. I'll have my phone on vibrate. Please call. It's important. I remember who answers the phone like Hank. Call me."

By the time of their first break, Kat had still not heard back from Jackson. Kat walked outside during the break to call Jackson. He still did not answer, so Kat looked around and left another message. "Jackson, call me back, please! It's Mrs. Judy. She answers the phone the exact same way as Hank. That's a very unusual way to answer the phone. Jackson, call me."

Mrs. Judy gave Kat a peculiar look as she walked back into the room. "What is Jackson up to today?" Mrs. Judy asked casually.

"Working," Kat answered.

"Is he still working with that ambulance company?" Mrs. Judy asked.

"Yes, ma'am," Kat answered.

"You have had a profound effect on him. He has stayed at jobs much longer at a time since the two of you got married," Mrs. Judy commented.

"I think that has more to do with budgeting than anything else," Kat replied.

"I think that you have more to do with it than you believe. Jackson really thinks the world of you," Mrs. Judy added.

Kat grinned and said, "Thank you. I like to think so at least." Was Mrs. Judy acting peculiar, or was that Kat's imagination? She had to get a hold of herself. It was hard to belief that Mrs. Judy would have anything to do with the terrorist sympathizers that Jackson was looking into, but if she was, then the last thing Kat wanted to do was tip Mrs. Judy off, especially when she couldn't get in touch with Jackson. If Kat couldn't calm down, she'd tip Mrs. Judy off quickly.

Kat took her seat. Everyone filed back in, and Mrs. Judy continued her presentation. The presentation was awesome, probably the best they had sat through thus far, but Mrs. Judy was way behind schedule. She was supposed to be finished by lunch; instead, she talked thirty minutes past the original time scheduled for lunch. She kept talking about an activity for them to try that would be great exercise physically, emotionally, and mentally. She never said exactly what type of activity. She gave away no details. Finally Mrs. Judy suggested that they break for lunch and come back after lunch for the activity. Everyone, of course, was in agreement, seeing that they were all so eager for lunch.

Kat tried to sneak out with the rest of the crowd. She wanted to try calling Jackson again, but Mrs. Judy caught her.

"Kat, hold up," Mrs. Judy called. "I need to talk to you."

Kat hung back. The room cleared out fast; everyone was more than ready for lunch. Lunch was almost an hour late, and no one was interested in sticking around to see what Kat and Mrs. Judy were up to. They only had an hour for lunch, and they had no intentions of wasting a single minute.

"I know that now is not the best time, but I don't see you much anymore since you and Jackson tied the knot. I haven't gotten an opportunity to talk to you. I wanted to talk with you about a new ministry outreach I've been looking into," Mrs. Judy said.

Hank Heart walked in followed by another big man. The second man was extremely muscular, a sort of Vin Diesel type but taller.

Kat tried to stay calm. She smiled and said, "Hello," to Hank. Then she turned back to Mrs. Judy. "That would be awesome. What's the outreach approach?" Kat asked cheerfully, trying to stay calm even though she was feeling anything but calm right now. What was Hank doing here, and what was going on? Where was Jackson, and why was he not returning her calls?

Hank pulled a chair out into the middle of the room while the second man shut the door and locked it.

"Have a seat, and I'll tell you all about it," Mrs. Judy said coldly.

"Why don't we talk about it over lunch? That hour flies by fast," Kat suggested still feigning ignorance.

"Have a seat, Kat," Mrs. Judy instructed. "Aren't you the least bit curious what Mr. Heart is doing here?"

Mrs. Judy picked up her purse out from underneath the podium. She reached inside and pulled out a hand gun. The bigger guy slid a table in front of the locked door. He put a second table upside down on top of the first.

"Have a seat," Mrs. Judy repeated.

Kat obediently sat down. Hank opened up a set of cabinets. He began taking out a lot of wires, a bunch of electronic panels, several rolls of black electrical tape, and a remote.

Hank took the remote to Mrs. Judy, who was still standing at the podium holding the gun straight at Kat.

The two men went to work right away. They taped up wires all around the room. Between each strand of wires, they connected an electric panel. Mrs. Judy stood at the podium while they worked. She did not move. She did not budge. She did not blink. She pointed the gun and stared at Kat.

In less than an hour, there were a couple people at the door. The door knob shook, but did not turn. The teachers stayed in the hall talking, but did not try further to get inside. As the crowd grew, the chatter outside the door grew louder. Eventually someone with a key came to the door. They unlocked the door. They turned the squeaky knob, but the door would not open due to the tables. Both tables were heavy, and together they were virtually immovable.

"Do you know what they are doing?" Mrs. Judy asked. She gestured with the gun at Hank and the bigger man.

"They're rigging the whole room to blow," Kat answered. She knew that much, and now she knew that Mrs. Judy was certifiable. She only wished she had figured that out before she got herself into this situation.

"That's right, very good," Mrs. Judy taunted using her very best and most patronizing teacher's voice.

"With all four of us in here," Kat added.

"Don't get smart, Kat. You can't afford it right now," Mrs. Judy warned. "Beans tie her up."

The bigger guy took some rope out of another cabinet and tied up Kat as he was instructed without a word. He tied her hands behind her back. He tied her upper body to the back of the chair. He tied both her feet to the legs of the chair. The ropes were tight enough that she had no wiggle room, no chance of escape, but they were not so tight that they hurt.

The whole time chatter outside the room continued to increase. Some were pounding on the door. Some were trying to knock it open. Help was so close. Kat could hear them. If only she could scream for one of them to call nine-one-one… but Mrs. Judy would shoot her before she could get the words out of her mouth. A gunshot would be sure to attract enough attention for a nine-one-one call, but the police would not get here in time to do her much good if she got herself shot point blank from such a short distance.

"Alright, let's get their attention," Mrs. Judy said.

"Get whose attention?" Kat asked.

"Don't push your luck, Kat," Mrs. Judy cautioned. "I like you; that's the only reason you are still here. I could have gotten results just as well by killing you, and face it, killing you would have been faster and much easier. I assume you know who your husband really works for."

"I do," Kat replied. There was no sense in playing dumb on that point now; Mrs. Judy obviously knew too.

"Then you've heard all about No-Deal-Johnson?" Mrs. Judy asked.

"I have not," Kat answered.

"Your precious Jackson is not what he seems. He tries to act like he's so kind and caring, but he's not. He has a reputation that precedes him. He will not compromise. He will not negotiate no matter what danger he puts himself or others in. It's like he's not scared of anything, but nothing lasts forever." Mrs. Judy paused. She pointed the gun up into the air and fired it. Dust and bits of plaster rained down from the ceiling.

The chatter from the hall immediately ceased. Everything went deadly silent only for a minute. The silence was followed by a heard of feet barreling down the hall like a continuous roll of thunder. There was a lot of screaming, but no discernible voices. All their racket muddled together to make a defining roar that was not at all intelligible.

"There now, it won't take long now before the police and your dear husband show up. No-Deal-Johnson is not scared and does not care, but I can change all that."

"What about you, Mrs. Judy?" Kat interrupted. "You go to church every time the doors are opened. You pretend to be such a good lady, but here you stand. I'm tied to a chair, and you have a gun pointed at me."

"Hank, gag her," Mrs. Judy instructed. She took a red scarf out of her purse and tossed it to Hank. Hank stuffed the scarf into Kat's mouth, pulled it tight, and tied it behind her head. "You don't get it do you, Kat? I found Johnson's weakness. He wouldn't let anything happen to you. He wouldn't be able to stand himself if he did. He loves you too much. He won't negotiate if he's in danger. He won't negotiate if hostages are in danger, but maybe, just maybe, he will negotiate if you are in danger," Mrs. Judy explained.

Minutes later the sound of sirens filled the air, but in the room where Kat was tied up there was an eerie silence.

The police surrounded the school. They made a run through the school to be sure that the school had been completely evacuated. Next they began to set up in the hall outside where Kat was being kept.

Kelley White was heading up the operation for the police. Kelley turned to a shorter man in a police uniform and said, "I want verification on who is in that room. I want to know how many. I want to know how many hostages. I want to know how many weapons. I want to know what kind of weapons, and I want to know now. Get moving!"

The shorter man ran off and started shouting orders to other officers.

Kelley turned to a slender officer and said, "I want to know the identity of everyone in that room and a background on each one. Go!" Then Kelley turned to a younger officer and said, "I want a negotiator here ASAP, and I want everyone outside questioned. Now, Rookie!" Kelley walked up to another officer, an older officer, and asked, "You were the first one on the scene?"

"Sure was," the older officer answered.

"What have we got?" Kelley asked.

"Well, when the teachers got back from lunch, the door was locked. When the principal got back with the key, he unlocked the door, but something was blocking the door. He and a couple of the male teachers tried knocking the door down. A few minutes later, they heard a gun shot. Everyone ran out of the school, and someone called us. The last two seen in there were the guest speaker, Judy McCleen, and a teacher at the school, Kat Johnson. They are both unaccounted for," the older officer retold.

"Kat? Did you say Kat Johnson?" Kelley asked.

"Yes, do you know her?" the older officer asked.

"Yeah, thanks," Kelley responded.

Kelley swiftly paced down the hall towards the main entrance as he started to shout. "Where is that rookie? I want answers now. Someone get me contact with anyone in that room!"

As Kelley made it to the front entrance, Jackson came running in. Kelley stopped him. "What are you doing here?"

"Move out of my way, White," Jackson ordered, but Kelley did not budge.

"Look, don't stick your nose where it doesn't belong. You're going to get someone killed. I'm the policeman. This is my job," Kelley growled.

"Not anymore," Jackson said as he pulled out a CIA badge and held it up in Kelley's face. "This is my case, and that is my wife in there. Get out of

my way, and stay out of the way."

Kelley stepped back with a stunned look across his face. Kelley chased Jackson down the hall back toward the conference room where Kat was. Jackson grabbed the arm of the officer closest to the door. "Do you have contact inside yet?" he asked.

"No, sir," the officer answered.

Jackson pulled a cell phone out of his pocket. "What are you doing?" Kelley asked.

"I'm doing what you couldn't," Jackson answered. "I'm going to make contact."

"How are you going to do that?" Kelley demanded.

"I'm going to call my wife," Jackson said as he pressed send and held the phone up to his ear.

"Do you hear that?" Mrs. Judy asked. "Vibrating, it's her phone. Beans, in her pocket, get it."

The bigger guy, Beans, dug into Kat's pocket and pulled out her phone. He took it to Mrs. Judy.

Mrs. Judy answered the phone, "Hi, Jackson."

"Mrs. Judy, where's Kat?" Jackson asked.

"She's sitting right in front of me," Mrs. Judy answered.

"I want to talk to her," Jackson demanded.

"I'm sorry, Jackson. That just can't happen. She's gagged right now. You know first hand how mouthy Kat can be," Mrs. Judy said.

"Why are you doing this? She was your friend. What happened?" Jackson asked.

"You're right, Jackson. She was one of my friends, but you happened. Jackson, you do know what I'm capable of, don't you?" Mrs. Judy asked, but Jackson did not respond. "Why don't you just give that a little thought, and I'll call you back from this phone in one hour," Mrs. Judy hung up before Jackson could say anything else.

Mrs. Judy looked at Kat and smirked. "He asked about you. It won't be long now."

Kat's phone began to vibrate again in Mrs. Judy's hand. Mrs. Judy stared down at the phone. "Stubborn man, isn't he?" she said glancing up at Kat. Then she answered the phone. "Jackson, I was supposed to call you not the other way around and not for an hour."

"I want to talk to my wife, Mrs. Judy. How am I supposed to contemplate what you're capable of and what I'm willing to do to get her out if I don't know for sure she's alive in there? You might have already killed her, or she might have had a bad morning and cut out early. She may not be in there at all. I really am going to need proof, Mrs. Judy. You understand," Jackson pushed.

"You already know that she's in here. There is no doubt in your mind, and you know that she is still alive for now. You don't need to talk to her. You don't need anything, but I don't see what it would hurt," Mrs. Judy started walking toward Kat. She untied the scarf and held the phone up to Kat's ear. "Say hello, Kat."

"Hello, Kat," Kat replied.

"Kat, don't get smart. Just do whatever she says. I'm right outside the door, and I'm doing everything I can to get to you. Are you OK?" Jackson asked.

"Yes," Kat answered.

"Have they hurt you?" Jackson asked.

"No."

"Is Hank in there?"

"Yes."

"Are there any more?"

"Yes."

"More than one?"

"No."

"Male?"

"Yes."

"Is he a big guy?"

"Yes."

"Just three of them?"

"Yes."

"OK, I love you"

"I love you too."

Mrs. Judy took the phone away from Kat's ear. She put it back to her own and said, "You have one hour. I'll call you." She hung up and walked back to the podium. Neither she nor either of the men put the gag back into Kat's mouth, but Kat did not utter a word.

A broad shouldered man with dark hair walked up to Jackson in the hall. "What took you so long?" Jackson asked. "She's got my wife in there."

"Since when do you have a wife?" the man asked.

"It really is reassuring to know that ya'll keep such a watchful eye on me. I've married, and she's being held hostage in that room," Jackson said pointing at the door. "There are three of them. One female, smaller frame, older lady. She's the ring leader. Two males, one's medium build, owns a construction company, relatively strong guy. The third one is a big guy. I have names on the first two Judy McCleen and Hank Heart. I've been following Heart a while. His background's clean. We need to run a background on McCleen. I've established contact through my wife's cell phone. I've talked to McCleen and my wife. The hostage is fine. She's tied up and gagged but not hurt. McCleen is going to call back in an hour with a list of demands."

"Do you have a plan?" the man asked.

"Yeah, see what the psycho wants and get my wife out of there before we do anything. Are you going to help or not? Find me someone with McCleen's background. Let's see what we can do about establishing a visual," Jackson replied.

"Look for the obvious," the man said. "Has anyone tried those windows?" The man pointed to a row of windows just below the ceiling looking into the room.

Jackson turned to the first cop he saw. "Can we get a ladder somewhere around here?"

"I'll get right on it," the cop answered and walked away.

Jackson looked down the hall and shouted, "White." He motioned with his fingers for Kelley to come.

Kelley walked down the hall to Jackson grumbling under his breath the whole way.

"Have we got a layout of the school yet?" Jackson asked.

"Not yet," Kelley replied.

"Well, what's the hold up? Let's get it, a layout, floor plans, a sketch, anything. Just get me something. I need it ten minutes ago. Go see what you can scrounge up," Jackson ordered.

Outside the room the sound of chatter was on the rise again. This time it was not mostly women's voices like before, but rather it was mostly men's voices. No doubt, it was the police and Jackson also.

Inside the room, however, was very quiet. Mrs. Judy leaned against the podium silently staring at Kat with the hand gun still pointed in Kat's general direction. Kat, still tied to the chair, stared back. Hank and Beans were huddled in an opposite corner quietly whispering. The conference room was a very large room in order to hold the entire staff. This made it very hard to hear Hank and Beans; in fact, it was hard to tell they were talking at all. The air had kicked on, but it was not all that loud either. There were no windows opening up outside. The only windows were next to the ceiling facing into the hall, which made it slightly easier to hear the chatter in the hall. Virtually the only noise inside the room was coming from the hall; it was most definitely the loudest noise in the room.

Kat was studying Mrs. Judy's every move. Mrs. Judy did not move much. Every so often she would shift her weight to the opposite foot. She glanced down at her watch from time to time. Other than that, she kept her eyes fixated on Kat, and Kat matched Mrs. Judy stare for stare.

Beans began pacing back and forth in the back of the room. Hank stood next to Mrs. Judy and stared at Kat. Mrs. Judy rolled her eyes at Hank and looked down at her watch. She picked up the cell phone up off the podium where she had laid it and began dialing Jackson's number.

One end of the hall got deathly quiet when Jackson's phone started ringing. "Mrs. Judy?" Jackson answered. "Is Kat OK?"

"Yes, yes. She's fine. Are we going to talk business, or are you still stuck on that?" Mrs. Judy asked.

"Of course, what do you want?" Jackson asked.

"I want troops out of Iraq," Mrs. Judy replied.

"I don't have that authority," Jackson responded.

"Then you better find someone who has the authority," Mrs. Judy threatened.

"That's not going to happen, but you already knew that. Didn't you, Mrs. Judy? You're talking about one hostage in one school in one city. She means the world to me, but no one else is going to compromise an entire nation for one hostage," Jackson said.

"You don't want your one hostage to die, now do you?" Mrs. Judy asked.

"Mrs. Judy, be reasonable. What do you really want? What is your point today?" Jackson asked.

"I'll call back in fifteen minutes. Be ready," Mrs. Judy said and hung up.

Immediately after Mrs. Judy terminated the connection two local PD's started down the hall with a ladder.

"What did she say?" the second agent asked.

"She wants me to pull troops out of Iraq," Jackson answered.

"She what!" the other man reacted. "Have you thought about getting a psychiatrist up here to try and talk her out?"

"She knows I can't do that," Jackson said shaking his head. "She's trying to mess with my head, and it's working." Jackson said getting gradually louder and more agitated until he was screaming the word working at the top of his lungs. He began rapidly pacing back and forth across the hall as the two PD's set up the ladder.

Two more police came down the hall. One was carrying a folding table. The other was carrying floor plans, pens, pencils, highlighters, and pins.

"What was that?" Hank asked as Mrs. Judy sat the phone back down on the podium.

"That was psychological warfare. He wants her back. Now I'm testing his limits with simple games," Mrs. Judy answered.

Mrs. Judy smiled when they heard Jackson screaming from the other side of the door.

Hank walked around behind Kat. He pulled her hair back off her shoulders, and started running his fingers through her hair. The touch made her cringe internally.

"It won't be long now, Kat. He's losing it out there," Mrs. Judy said emotionlessly. "This will all be over soon enough."

Hank continued playing with Kat's hair. Was this Hank's version of psychological warfare, or was it simply due to the fact that he was a womanizing creep? Either way it didn't matter much; the end result was still the same. Kat wanted to break everyone of his fingers for touching her without her permission.

Jackson was studying the floor plans when his phone started ringing. "Hello," he answered.

"Listen closely. I have five demands," Mrs. Judy said.

"Someone get me something to write on," Jackson called. He was already holding a pencil in hand.

"Are we not ready, Johnson?" Mrs. Judy asked.

Jackson made a face. He angrily flipped the floor plans over where the backside was showing. "I'm ready. Talk business," he said.

"Number one, I want a name."

"What's wrong with Judy?" Jackson asked.

"Don't get funny. I want the name of the guy who killed John Smith," Mrs. Judy clarified.

"Who?" Jackson responded.

"Don't play dumb with me. You know exactly who I'm talking about," Mrs. Judy snapped.

"The assassin?" Jackson asked. "The one who tried to assassinate the president?"

"Intentional assassin," Mrs. Judy corrected.

"How would I know that?" Jackson asked.

"You'll figure it out," Mrs. Judy answered.

"Number two," Jackson pushed.

"Number two, I want thirty-six million put into my account."

"So that it can disappear into an untraceable account two minutes after we deposit it," Jackson commented. A lot of money, this psycho had her so-called ideals, and she had pure old fashioned greed.

"See, you're not as dumb as you try to pretend," Mrs. Judy replied.

"Great, number three," Jackson continued.

"Number three, you leave town and don't come back."

"Perfect, I can't wait," Jackson responded. "Number four."

"Number four, you clear this whole place out. When we get ready to leave, there is not a soul within a two mile radius of this school."

"Fine, what's number five?" Jackson urged.

"Number five, Beans is left alone. He gets out of this scot-free. He has no idea what's going on. He's just doing what he's being told. All brute, no brains," Mrs. Judy said.

"I'll see what I can do. Is that all?" Jackson asked.

"That's it. I'll call back in ten minutes," Mrs. Judy replied.

"I can't do that. I need more than ten minutes," Jackson insisted.

"We'll see what happens," Mrs. Judy said and then hung up.

Jackson slammed the phone down on the table. He looked up at the second agent. He slapped the list of demands and said, "Make it happen."

"What?" the man reacted with confusion. "What happened to No-Deal-Johnson?"

Jackson shoved the man hard against a wall and pressed his forearm sharply into the man's throat. "That's my wife in there with a gun pointed at her head. When it's your wife in there, then you can lecture me on negotiating. Until then this is still my case; we do things my way. Make it happen."

The man walked back to the table as soon as Jackson let go. He started looking over the list. "Johnson," he called pointing to number one on the list.

Jackson glanced down at the list then looked the man in the face. The man raised his eyebrows and shrugged his shoulders. "What did you want me to do?" Jackson asked. "Did you want me to tell her I know who did it, because I did it myself? She would have killed Kat without a moment's hesitation then blown this whole area sky high… White!" Jackson hollered.

"What?" Kelley answered grudgingly.

"With confirmation of several bombs in that room, I suppose that you are prepared to evacuate this area," Jackson said.

"Yeah so," Kelley responded.

"Good, good. On my signal you clear every living creature in a two mile radius," Jackson instructed. Then he turned back to the second agent. "You just get that money ready to go."

Jackson walked over to the ladder. "You," he said pointing to the agent up at the window, "Come down. I'm coming up."

The hall was crawling now with men wearing CIA badges around their neck. The man on top of the ladder climbed down. Jackson grabbed the phone off the table and climbed the ladder.

Mrs. Judy was standing at the front of the room behind a podium holding a gun. Five separate bombs were strapped half way up the walls all the way around the room. The bigger man, who must have been Beans, was off to himself. Kat was tied to a chair directly in front of Mrs. Judy. Hank was standing behind Kat messing with her hair.

Jackson was still on the ladder peering in the window when his phone began to ring. "Yeah," he answered.

"Well?" Mrs. Judy asked.

"I need more time to get the money and take care of Beans," Jackson said as Hank moved his hands down to Kat's shoulders and started rubbing her shoulders. "Tell Heart to keep his hands off my wife, or all deals are off when I come through this window to kill him," Jackson quickly added.

Mrs. Judy glanced up at the window. "How nice of you to join us, Johnson."

"Tell him, Mrs. Judy," Jackson insisted.

"Hank, let the girl go," Mrs. Judy instructed. "What have you got so far, Johnson?"

Hank dropped his hands to the chair back.

"I'll give you the name after you give me Kat. I have men getting the money together as we speak. As soon as Kat is back in my arms, I'm headed straight to the house to pack my bags. Everyone for two miles is ready to evacuate on my signal. I'm still working on Beans. I'll be honest with you. I don't know what else I can do, but even so, as long as he is truly clueless, he has a good chance at an insanity plea," Jackson explained.

"I suggest you try harder," Mrs. Judy said.

"I've got my eye on Heart," Jackson warned before Mrs. Judy hung up.

Jackson looked down at the second agent. "Patterson, get me some explosives."

"What for?" Patterson asked.

"Get them just in case," Jackson answered.

For a long time Jackson ignored everything going on below him as he watched through the window, but no one inside moved. After a while Kat began to speak, but Jackson could not hear through the glass.

"Mrs. Judy, what happens if Jackson can't meet all the demands?" Kat asked softly.

"He cares for you too much to find out. He'll meet them," Mrs. Judy answered.

"What if he doesn't have the power to meet them all?" Kat asked.

"I wouldn't worry that pretty little face too much about that," Hank said stroking Kat's cheek and grinning.

Jackson started banging on the window with his fist. Everyone in the room with the exception of Kat looked up at the window. Jackson held his hand up like a gun and pointed at Hank. Hank smiled up, and Jackson pretended to pull the trigger.

"I've got the explosives, and I've got the money. It's ready to deposit on my word," Patterson hollered up.

"Set the explosives around the door. Make sure it's enough to take down the door and the two tables behind the door," Jackson replied. Then he called Mrs. Judy back.

"Give me your spiel," Mrs. Judy answered.

"Your money is ready. How do you want to do this?" Jackson blurted out.

Hank pulled a chair over and sat down right next to Kat. "What about Beans?" Mrs. Judy asked.

"What about him?" Jackson asked. "I've done everything I can for Beans. There's nothing else within my power to do. That is another one of those requests that goes over my authority, and I'm the highest rank you're going to get for a one hostage situation."

"And if that's not good enough?" Mrs. Judy asked.

"It will have to be good enough. I've done all I could. I took care of everything else. This is supposed to be a negotiation, isn't it? I give a little, you give a little," Jackson said.

"I think I'm already giving a lot. I'm giving you Kat," Mrs. Judy reminded.

Hank reached over and laid his palm high on Kat's thigh and squeezed. Jackson pulled his gun. He hit the window with his gun shattering the glass. He reached inside the window and aimed his gun straight at Hank's head. Jackson tensed up ready to pull the trigger, but jerked his arm back instead. He slid down the ladder holding onto the sides. "Are those explosives ready?" Jackson asked talking to anyone who would answer.

"Hank, get away from her," Mrs. Judy shouted and started franticly calling Jackson back.

"We're ready to trade," Mrs. Judy jumped before Jackson had a chance to say a word.

"Ready," an agent answered.

"Too late," Jackson said into the phone and dropped it to the ground. "Blast it," he told the agent.

One agent holding a remote started to shout, "Alright people, three, two, one."

The door exploded. Jackson did not wait for the rubble to clear. He ran straight through the falling debris into the conference room and put a bullet into the shoulder of a very stunned Judy McCleen.

Mrs. Judy lost her balance and fell down. Jackson put his right foot on Mrs. Judy's injured shoulder applying slight pressure. "Don't move," he ordered. Then he pointed his gun at Hank who had pulled a pocket knife. "Drop the knife," Jackson shouted. Hank dropped the knife promptly. "Untie her," Jackson instructed as four more agents including Patterson poured into the room.

Hank untied Kat from the chair. She hopped immediately to her feet. She executed a sweep kick to knock Hank's feet out from underneath him. Hank collapsed to the floor, and Kat kicked him swiftly in the side of his abdomen.

"Kat," Jackson called as Patterson was handcuffing Mrs. Judy and reading her rights. Another agent was handcuffing Hank and reading his rights. "Kat, that's enough," Jackson said. He walked over to Kat and Hank. He looked down at Hank. He smiled and said, "I told you to keep you hands off my wife." Then he put his gun away, took Kat in his arms, and kissed her. "I love you," he said.

"Can we go home now?" Kat asked holding back tears.

"Yeah, let's go home," Jackson smiled.

# Chapter 13

Jackson drove Kat home, and they left her car at the school. Jackson pulled his truck around to the back of the house into the carport. He helped Kat out of the truck, and they started toward the back door.

Kat grabbed Jackson's arm. "Wait," she said. "Jackson, I knocked that plant over this morning." Kat pointed at a potted plant sitting on the porch next to the door. "I was running late, so I just left it. I was going to clean it up when I got home. Dirt was everywhere."

Jackson looked at the plant. It was sitting next to the door up against the side of the house. The porch was clean. There was no dirt or debris anywhere."

"Are you sure?" Jackson asked.

"Positive," Kat answered.

"Go back to the truck and lock the doors," Jackson instructed. He pulled out his gun. He slowly unlocked the door and eased it open.

Kat locked herself in the truck. Jackson quietly crept inside. He went through every room carefully checking for anything out of the ordinary.

Jackson had not been inside long when a couple exited through the same door Jackson had entered. They looked to be in their early to mid sixties. They spotted Kat right away and started straight for the truck. The man picked up a rock. He busted the window out on the passenger side while the lady walked over to the driver's side. There was no where for Kat to go, so she honked the horn. The man reached inside the truck and unlocked the doors. He opened the door, reached across the seats, and grabbed Kat's arm.

The man was pulling Kat out of the car when Jackson came running out of the house. Jackson had his gun aimed at the man and almost pulled the trigger before he stopped himself, but he did stop himself just in the nick of time. He lowered his gun and put it away.

"My truck!" Jackson screamed when he noticed the window. "Mr. Cook, what are you doing? Have you lost your mind? Let her go. Look. You're scaring her."

The man let go of Kat's arm. Kat ran to Jackson. "It's OK," Jackson whispered.

"Let's talk about this inside. I don't want to alarm the neighbors," the man said.

"Come on," Jackson said, and he led Kat inside.

The couple followed Jackson and Kat inside and shut the door.

"What do you want?" Jackson asked.

"Why couldn't you take no for an answer?" the lady asked.

"Why couldn't you?" Jackson retaliated. "You're not welcome here. Just go home."

"That's my little girl. You have no right to tell me I can't see her," the man shouted.

Kat, who was still holding onto Jackson's arm, froze in her tracks. "Oh, I'm sorry. Kat, this is Mr. and Mrs. Cook. They are your parents. Mr. and Mrs. Cook, this is Kat."

"I don't need you to introduce me to my own daughter," Mrs. Cook snapped.

"Get out," Kat ordered boldly.

"Calm down, sweetheart. I didn't mean to scare you. We just came to check on you," Mr. Cook said.

"Don't call me sweetheart. I am calm. You weren't here when I needed you. You have no business here now. Get out," Kat ordered again.

"We did what we had to," Mrs. Cook said.

"That's right," Mr. Cook interjected. "We did. We didn't want you mixed up in this whole thing. That's why we left you with your aunt." Mr. Cook shot an evil look in Jackson's direction. "I thought we had separated you two, but you just couldn't stand leaving her out of this."

"You did separate us. You did an excellent job. It wasn't until after I had given up on Melissa that I met Kat. What I don't understand is why. I love your daughter. I always have. I would do anything for her. Just tell me why," Jackson pushed.

"To keep her from getting involved in the very thing you pulled her into," Mrs. Cook said.

"Jane," Mr. Cook interrupted.

"It doesn't matter now. When McCleen told us about you and Kat James, we thought you had finally started to move on. You were forgetting all about Melissa, so we told McCleen to push it. I thought we had finally succeeded in prying you away when McCleen reported that you had gone through with the wedding. Imagine our shock when we found out that Kat James was our Melissa. Imagine my disappointment to find out you took Rudy's last name. I have no one to blame but myself. We never should have trusted an amateur like McCleen," Mrs. Cook said.

"You're behind this all?" Jackson asked in obvious disbelief.

"Listen, Jackson, we never meant for it to come down to you, son. It was just bad luck when you got assigned to this case," Mr. Cook explained.

"You just told me that you are involved in the largest terrorist action since nine-eleven, and you expect me to believe that you never intended me to get burnt. Bull, and what about Kat? When you joined forces with terrorist, you were gunning after every American including Kat," Jackson pointed out.

"I don't care what you did or why. I don't care who you are, and I don't care to find out. All I want is for you to get out of my house," Kat said.

"Do you see what you've done?" Mr. Cook snapped at Jackson. "You've turned my only child against us."

"No!" Kat shouted losing her temper. "Jackson didn't do that. You did that. You did that when you abandoned me. You never visited. You never called. You never even wrote. The only thing I remember about you is how you were always gone. I don't remember anything about my life before you left, and I don't remember Melissa. I hate you, and that is not his fault. I've hated you for years, long before I met Jackson."

A knock at the front door interrupted Kat. "Ignore it. They'll go away," Mrs. Cook said.

Kat knocked a vase to the floor, shattering the vase. She picked up a gun that Jackson kept hidden in the bottom of the vase and pointed it at the Cooks. "Get out!" she shouted.

"You wouldn't dare," Mrs. Cook challenged.

Kat fired a shot above her head and shouted again, "Get out!"

There was a loud crash in the front of the house as pieces of the ceiling fell from the gun shot.

"It's Mommy and Daddy, sweetheart. We would never hurt you intentionally," Mr. Cook pleaded.

"Get out," Kat repeated.

"Freeze! No one goes anywhere," Patterson shouted as he entered the room with his gun already aimed at the Cooks. "Put your guns on the ground and your hands in the air." Patterson tossed a pair of cuffs at Jackson. "Start cuffing them. Back up is on the way."

"That's my in-laws, man," Jackson protested.

"The in-laws? Really? That's great. They are my mentors. Cuff them," Patterson argued stonily.

Jackson started cuffing Mrs. Cook first. Six agents barged in. The first one cuffed Mr. Cook. The second read Mr. Cook his rights. The third read Mrs. Cook her rights. The other three secured the premises. Within only minutes Mr. and Mrs. Cook were being drug out, and Jackson, Kat, and Patterson were left standing alone.

"How did you know?" Jackson asked.

"It was the bigger suspect back at the school. He started going on and on about how the girl's parents said to protect her. I had a bad feeling that this might not be over. When I got here and saw your busted truck window, I called for back up. I've got to tell you though. I heard the shot, but I wasn't prepared to walk in here and see Mark and Jane." Patterson explained.

"I never saw that one coming either. They taught me so much growing up," Jackson admitted.

"I'm not surprised at all," Kat complained.

Jackson tried to force a laugh and hugged Kat close.

## About the Author

Elizabeth Lee Sorrell is an Alabama native. A gifted teacher, she has worked with babies and preschoolers, from her teens all the way to today. She is a teacher in the Federal Head Start program. She has her Associate's Degree in Early Childhood Development, her Bachelor's in Early Childhood Education and Elementary Education, and her Master's in Early Childhood Education.

When not teaching, or leading as the Nursery Coordinator of her church, she is with her family and dear friends, probably reading or writing a book. She loves to spend time with her nieces. Elizabeth is a Christian. She cheers for the Auburn Tigers, and the Atlanta Braves. As a big baseball fan, she has, more than once, written stories in the world of MLB, and watches as many games as she is able.

She enjoys pairing up with Sandra JS Coleman for her covers and illustrations. Sandra, Elizabeth's sister, is a graphic designer and an artist-illustrator.

Learn more at www.ElizabethLeeSorrell.com

## Colophon

Cover and interior layout designed by
Sandra JS Coleman using Adobe CC software.

The typefaces used on the cover and interior are
American Typewriter and Minion Pro, as well as
Skippy Sharp.

Minion was designed by Robert Slimbach in 1990 as a
digital typeface for Adobe Systems, inspired by late
Renaissance-era typography. Minion Pro is an
OpenType Update. It was released in 2000.

Skippy Sharp, drawn by Skippy McFadden in 1995, was
completed by typographer, Chank Diesel.

The book was printed in the United States of America,
on 50lb creme paper, perfect bound, with a gloss cover.